The Silver Notebook

Enda Wyley

THE O'BRIEN PRESS
DUBLIN

First published 2007 by The O'Brien Press Ltd,
12 Terenure Road East, Rathgar, Dublin 6, Ireland.
Tel: +353 1 4923333; Fax: +353 1 4922777
E-mail: books@obrien.ie
Website: www.obrien.ie

ISBN 978-1-84717-020-0

The quotation from *Four Quartets*, T. S. Eliot, is reprinted
with the permission of Faber and Faber Ltd.

British Library Cataloguing-in-publication Data
Wyley, Enda, 1966-
The silver notebook
1. Fathers and sons - Juvenile fiction 2. Authors - Juvenile fiction
3. Children's stories
I. Title
823.9'14[J]

1 2 3 4 5 6 7 8 9 10
07 08 09 10 11 12 13 14 15

The O'Brien Press receives
assistance from

the arts
council
schomhairle
ealaíon

Printed by Cox and Wyman Ltd.

DEDICATION
For my daughter, Freya Sirr

Acknowledgements

Special thanks go to my niece Iseult O'Rourke, this book's first enthusiastic and helpful reader. I am enormously grateful to Íde ní Laoghaire at The O'Brien Press for her wise editing of this story. Many thanks! Love and gratitude must also go to my husband, Peter Sirr, my parents and my brothers and sisters. Finally, I am indebted to the Irish Arts Council for granting me a Literature Bursary to complete this book and to Clíodhna ní Anluain for broadcasting parts of it on *Fiction 15, Stories for Children*, RTÉ 1.

'And the end of all our exploring

Will be to arrive where we started

And know the place for the first time.'

From *Four Quartets*, T. S. Eliot

Contents

Prologue

Timothy Finn had no father – well, he did have one, but he had never met him. His father left his mother just before Timothy was born. Nobody knew why, or where his Dad had gone.

Then on Timothy's eighth birthday a present arrived, something small but special. Something that would change Timothy's life forever. Just what this mysterious present was, just how important it was to become in Timothy's search for his father, this story will tell – along with many other things besides.

But first, let's start where all stories should.

At the beginning.

Chapter 1

Timothy Finn

Timothy Finn had a special gift. You see, for as long as he could remember he had always loved words.

As a small baby he loved the sound of the words he could hear everywhere. He loved the way they fell in spurts from the large mouths of adults buzzing around him. Most especially, Timothy loved his mum's words because they flapped happily through the house, like beautiful singing birds.

And when his mother would wrap him up in his pram and take him for a walk down by the pier, Timothy could even understand what the seagulls were cawing about.

They swooped in search of fish, calling out: 'Hey, look! There's baby Timothy Finn. We haven't seen him for a while! Let's say hello.'

Then they would flap over Timothy's head, creating such a massive flurry with their wings that nearby fishermen would stop their work at the nets and stare. They had never seen so many birds surround a young child! And frightened by the seagulls' sudden appearance, Julia would drop her book and wave her arms at them.

'Leave my little boy alone! Go away, you nasty things!' called Julia.

Only Timothy knew they were just being friendly. He wanted to speak to them, but knew he couldn't, so he just wiggled his fingers and toes at them, smiling as they flew away.

As he grew older, Timothy came to love even more that words could be used to make up stories. People believed you, they listened to you, they wanted to hear more.

In fact, from an early age Timothy Finn became a very good storyteller exactly because he loved the reaction he got from everyone around him.

❈   ❈   ❈

One day, when Timothy was five years old, he found a shiny coin on the way to Rowanstown, the village he had lived in since he was a small baby. He immediately ran as fast as he could to Rosie's shop.

'Hi, Rosie! Guess what happened?'

'I don't know. You tell me, young Mr Finn.' Rosie always called him 'young Mr Finn' and this made Timothy smile.

'Well, I was very busy this morning–'

'I can well imagine,' Rosie interrupted. She liked to do that too, but Timothy wasn't put off.

'–when I heard an enormous crash!' Timothy's eyes grew large and he moved in closer to Rosie. 'A car had smashed into a tree, just a tiny bit away from me. I was very lucky, you know.'

'And was everyone okay?' Rosie looked interested now. The story was working.

'Actually, yes. A policeman came by and phoned an

ambulance and the driver and his wife were taken away. But they seemed okay.'

'What a relief,' Rosie said.

'Yes, but then, when they were all gone, I noticed something.'

'What?' Rosie leaned in towards Timothy. It had been a very quiet morning with few customers and she was delighted with the gossip.

'Well, an old lady on the other side of the road was so upset by the crash that she dropped all her shopping and looked really ill. So, I ran over and helped her put everything back in her bag and then offered to carry her bags home for her.'

'Poor woman,' Rosie said. 'Where does she live? Maybe I know her?'

'Oh, I don't think so.' Timothy hoped the story wouldn't be ruined by Rosie catching him out. 'Anyway, she wanted to walk home by herself so I don't know where she lives. But before she went she gave me this!' Timothy held the gleaming coin up in front of Rosie.

'Wasn't that kind of her.' Rosie clapped her hands in delight. 'Well now, young Mr Finn, you will have to buy some sweets with that. And do you know what? I think I'll throw in extra ones for you too on account of you being so kind to that poor old thing.'

'Oh, please don't, Rosie! I'm happy with what I can get with this.'

'Well, if you're sure,' Rosie said. 'What a nice boy you are!'

Later, when Julia came into the shop, Rosie said: 'Such a kind, polite boy you have there in Timothy. Just like you were at that age, I'd imagine!' and she winked, making Julia blush.

Julia wasn't sure she liked Rosie making comments about her. She was a very private person.

* * *

Timothy smiled all the way home. His stories weren't really lies, he told himself, they were just made-up half-truths that others believed. They didn't cause anyone any harm, after all, and they were fun to tell.

He hummed as he strolled along. He loved his little village. It was called Rowanstown because all the streets were lined with rowan trees and Timothy loved following the winding streets out beyond the pier to the cliff path where Boat Cottage, his home, shaped exactly like a boat, could be seen shining like a bright jewel dug deep into the peninsula.

His mum had bought the cottage when Timothy was just a few weeks old and they had left the city behind – just the two of them – to set up a new life together in Rowanstown. She had decorated the entire place, taking care to make a studio for herself below the deck. For Julia Finn was a painter and there was nothing she loved more than to sit, her easel facing the waves below, and to sketch and paint all day.

❉　❉　❉

Rowanstown was full of great places to play and Timothy loved to climb the mountains, to run down to the beach or to go to the harbour and talk to his friends, the fisher-men, there. Julia would wave him off in the morning and then go to her studio to paint for several hours. She liked to work there because the wide, large windows always gave her a good view of where Timothy was every time she looked up from her easel. Rowanstown was also a very safe place and everyone knew Timothy, so Julia never worried about him.

Then, around midday, she would see him climbing up the hill to Boat Cottage. Every lunchtime, Timothy came home hungry and bursting with stories. And Julia looked forward to hearing them.

'So, I was sitting at the edge of the pier with my fish-ing rod, just chatting to Gregory, when I felt the most enormous pull on the line.'

'Lucky you that Gregory was there. He's such an experienced fisherman,' Julia said, pouring Timothy another glass of delicious blueberry and mango juice. Storytelling was thirsty work.

'Exactly,' Timothy continued. 'So, I pulled and

pulled. Whatever it was felt huge, Mum. I pulled and pulled! My arms *still* feel sore from it all. Then Gregory had to hang on to my waist and pull and pull too. Then it got so bad that Owen jumped out of his boat and he held on to Gregory who was hanging on to me and then all of us had to pull. Then Mrs Cummins was walking her dog and she came by and she decided to help. She hung on to Owen and we all pulled. Her dog was barking like mad!'

Julia was laughing now, flicking her curly hair back from her eyes. She loved the way Timothy told a story.

'Then, suddenly, the line broke and we all fell down on the pier. Mrs Cummins had her knitting in her bag and the wool rolled out and all the seagulls went after it, pecking and making lots of noise. I had to chase them away. It was funny.' Timothy was laughing now too, enjoying his tale. He was even beginning to believe it himself. 'One of the gulls flew away with half of the jumper she was knitting! Mrs Cummins didn't like that!'

'I'm sure she didn't. She prides herself on her knitting. But what happened to your line? It looks fine to me.' Julia looked at Timothy's fishing rod standing by the kitchen door.

'Oh, Gregory fixed it for me.' Timothy bent his head down and bit into his cheese sandwich, mayonnaise dripping from his mouth.

'And what was it in the sea that had been so heavy?' Julia wanted to know some more.

That was the problem with stories, Timothy thought, you had to work so hard to make people believe them. They wanted to know every single detail. You needed to be very careful if you wanted to be a good storyteller.

'Well, that's the best part.' Timothy looked up at her, his eyes gleaming. He had thought of an exciting ending that he knew his mum would love.

'While everyone was busy dusting themselves down I looked over the pier into the sea and saw the most amazing thing. A long, long fish, the brightest blue you've ever seen, with gold and green spots on it and a silver tail. It was so beautiful that I started to jump up and down and point at it and Gregory came running. He said he'd never in all his days of fishing seen such a thing. He thought maybe because the sea was warmer recently that it had come from some faraway land. It swam all the way from Africa to our little village of Rowanstown. Imagine!'

'Imagine …' Julia's voice trailed away, the way it always did when she was making a plan. 'All the way from Africa. What a wonderful painting that would make … a fish with golden and green spots and a tail tipped with silver. A beautiful, magical thing … yes, I think I know what to do …'

And off she headed to her studio, her fingers itching to paint, her lunch left uneaten. Timothy finished it for her. He was always hungry.

If Timothy was good at telling stories, Julia was just as good at making paintings. Boat Cottage was always full of ideas. Soon a wonderful fish hung over the fireplace, the paint thick and bright and glowing. And if anyone who came to visit asked about it, Julia told them proudly, 'That's the fish that Timothy very nearly caught.'

Chapter 2

Timothy's Private Story

There was one story Timothy told that Julia didn't like.

'Timothy! Who are you talking to?' Julia came upon her little boy one day chatting away to himself. He was standing in the middle of the trees at the back of Boat Cottage, bluebells all around him, his head tilted upwards as though there was actually somebody there.

'My dad. We often have talks. About everything, really. He's going to take me out in a boat soon with Gregory and we're going to have a picnic. He loves sandwiches and crisps and lemonade. And we're going to stop off at Rowanstown Island and have our picnic there and then play hide and seek in the grave-yard and–'

'Your Dad! The graveyard! No, Timothy. Please, you

mustn't talk like this. Haven't you been happy, just the two of us? Come on, now, enough of that silly talk. You know how I told you your Dad had to go away.'

'But he might come back, right?' Timothy stared up at Julia, his eyes full of hope.

'Of course he might.' Julia forced a smile. 'But we're doing fine just as we are, aren't we?' and she hugged her little boy tight.

※　※　※

After that day among the bluebells, Julia Finn made a decision. Timothy spent too much time alone. He needed friends. He was five years of age and Julia decided it was time to start him at Rowanstown national school.

It was a red-bricked, high-windowed old building full of local children. And Timothy really liked his teacher, Miss Cornellie. Her name suited her because her first name was Nell and her hair was yellow, like corn. She was a tall, handsome woman, always smiling and fun to be with.

On his first day at school, when Julia waved good-bye, Miss Cornellie bent down to look into his eyes and Timothy was immediately won over by her kind face.

'Timothy Finn. At last! I've been waiting for you. You remind me of your mum when she was little! Come in, come in.' She pointed inside to the bright room full of smiling five-year-old faces.

'My mum? Did you know her?' Timothy asked.

'Oh yes, a long time ago. We were friends. I'm sure she'll tell you all about it sometime.'

Timothy smiled back at his teacher, but quickly forgot about what she had said. He had lots to do – like making cakes out of playdough, finishing a giant jigsaw puzzle on the floor or painting a yellow sun.

Pretty soon school began to fill up his days and Timothy came to love going there and finding in his classroom, with Miss Cornellie's help, new things to learn and do.

Years went by and Timothy never mentioned his father to Julia again. Julia Finn was delighted to see her son growing happier and happier each day – that is, until Timothy's eighth birthday, when things began to change.

Chapter 3

Things Begin to Change

Now, every child loves Christmas and Timothy was no exception, especially because it was also his birthday. So, while most children were opening their presents from Santa, Timothy had *two* sets of gifts to enjoy – his Christmas and his birthday ones.

And while most families in Rowanstown were having turkey and ham, potatoes and Brussels sprouts for dinner, Timothy was allowed have whatever he wanted to eat on his birthday.

On his eighth birthday Julia cooked Timothy's favourite for that year: Bats' Wings followed by Beautiful Butterflies. Julia always made up great names for the food she made in the kitchen, which she called the Cooking Cabin. Chicken wings were turned over in a baking tray and cooked in soy sauce, molasses and ginger, then served dripping in the dark sauce. Timothy loved them. For dessert, Julia cut thin pastry into butterfly shapes and covered them in colourful little chocolate sweets, so that they looked exactly like the delicate butterflies Timothy always admired in the fields around Boat Cottage.

Well and truly stuffed and happy, Timothy and Julia went downstairs to the studio. There, beside the roaring fire, Timothy opened his presents. He was having a great birthday.

The vases on the tables and the mantelpiece were filled with holly branches with red berries, mistletoe and green leaves. A fresh smell filled the room. Julia's face glowed in the firelight and Timothy thought he had never felt so happy.

'Happy birthday, Timothy!' his mum half-sang, and she handed him a parcel. 'Eight today!'

It was a beautiful fountain pen, engraved with a tiny heart and the words *Love, Julia* along its silver lid.

Nobody else he knew called their mother by her first

name as Timothy sometimes did, and he was glad to see her name there now. He would treasure this present forever. And there were other gifts too.

Santa must have known they had a studio in Boat Cottage because he gave Timothy a new set of paints and paper and an easel all for himself, and just the right size too.

'We can have an exhibition together,' Julia laughed. 'Come on! Let's start some new paintings now.'

But then she turned back, her face going pale, her fingers pulling at her hair distractedly. Timothy saw how her hands were shaking.

'Oh, I forgot something. This came for you a few days ago. I'm not sure who it's from … although the handwriting … I'm sure it's someone I know. It's so familiar …' She looked vague, unhappy.

Julia handed Timothy a small, thick package. 'Open it,' she said, pushing the bulky envelope into Timothy's hand and turning her back to him as he began to tear the paper apart.

Why were Julia's shoulders shuddering and why was she sniffling? Or was it that she knew something more about this present, but for some reason she just wasn't saying?

When the gift fell on the floor with a thud, Julia turned around with a start and cried out, 'What is it? What is it?'

Timothy had never seen her so upset. Something strange was happening.

'Julia! Mum! Don't worry, it's only a notebook. But a beautiful one.'

Timothy ran his fingers along its smooth cover. It was covered in a silver material and was smooth to touch. Inside, the paper was thick, yellow and unlined.

It was then he saw the writing.

> And the end of all our exploring
>
> Will be to arrive where we started
>
> And know the place for the first time.

The lines were scrawled in thick black print across the first page with a big 'X' and 'From Dad' below it.

'What does it mean?' Timothy heard himself speak, his voice sounding pinched and worried. When he looked up, his mum's face was white and frightened-looking.

'It's ... it's a poem. I've seen it before.' Julia's voice was quiet now.

'Where did you see it?' Timothy wanted to know.

'Well, it's a poem ... It was your father's favourite ... he loved to read it and write it down. Those lines are from a poem by a man who wrote a long time ago, a man called Eliot …'

But the last thing Timothy wanted to hear about was a poet, especially when *his father* had just sent him something – *his father*, who had never sent him anything. The father he never knew.

'No, I mean, my *dad*? My dad sent me this? But I've never met him. Where is he? Mum, what does it all mean?' Great tears were filling his eyes and

Timothy couldn't stop them falling.

It was then that Julia, cuddling her son close to her, told the story she had kept a secret from him until he was old enough to really understand. That day in the blue-bells, he was too young. But Julia knew that now the time was right.

Chapter 4

The Big Secret

This is the story that Julia told her eight-year-old son, Timothy.

❋   ❋   ❋

It was the winter that nobody wore hats or coats or scarves or gloves. The weather was so mild that weeks upon weeks went by in mid-December when people even wore sandals. Everyone looked happy. They walked down the streets smiling, their faces freckled in the sun, their skin a golden brown.

How strange, unexpected it seemed, then, when, just a week before Christmas, a heavy fall of snow covered the world in a fluffy white. It took the weathermen by surprise, closed schools, brought traffic to a standstill, sent people rummaging for the woollens they had so happily folded away. Everyone grew grumpy. Everyone, that is, except Julia Finn.

Julia had hated the sun. She was pregnant and found it uncomfortable to be hot and heavy in the middle of December. She wanted the cold back. She wanted evenings snuggled up by the fire, eating marshmallows and reading. Her baby was due in just a few weeks and this strange sun made her cross, her skin blotchy, her temperature rise and her feet swell. Where was winter gone? A terrible feeling began to creep through her. Something awful was going to happen. She knew it. And the more she thought about it, the more she convinced herself she was right.

But then the snow came. A cold, fresh air blew through the city and Julia Finn heaved a sigh of relief. Everything would be all right, after all. Only later would she realise just how wrong she had been. The snow came and Julia's life was to change forever.

Julia Finn would never forget that afternoon. Trains

and buses had been forced to stop due to the heavy pile-up of snow. Taxis were full and Julia found herself walking the three miles from the city to her house.

It was hard at first, as she felt tired with the weight of the baby inside her. But soon her body relaxed into a comfortable rhythm and Julia began to enjoy the clear air, the look of the enormous snow clouds filling the sky, the way her skin tingled in the cold.

When she reached her gate she was filled with a huge happiness and wanted to tell her husband exactly how she felt. She pushed the front door open and called out his name, but there was only silence.

'Hello, hello!' She began to shout now, but still nobody answered. Only the floorboards creaked.

Then she saw the note.

Just gone out for a while. Maybe will pick up that baby bath you wanted? Am sorry for being so cross. See you soon. X

Julia sighed. She knew he had been upset that morning. But he must have cheered up. He'd be back soon, she thought. Still, she felt there was something he wasn't telling her, some kind of secret.

After all, they had a lot to be excited about. Their baby was soon to be born. If it was a boy, Julia had already decided on a name: Timothy.

The afternoon stretched on. Evening came. Darkness fell, but still Julia's husband did not come home. She lit the fire and made dinner for two. She waited and waited. But the garden gate never clicked open, nobody turned the key in the front door.

Julia tried not to worry. They had argued before and he had always come back. This time would be the same.

She ate her half of the food and at midnight threw out the rest – it had gone cold and soggy.

Outside, the temperature was dropping. The snow froze and looked an icy blue. Julia piled more blankets on her bed and rolled in under them. She slept in fits and starts through that night. Finally, hot and worried, she pulled on her dressing gown and went downstairs to make herself a drink.

She loved hot chocolate. That would relax her.

Day was beginning to break. A cluster of birds chirped outside the kitchen window and pecked at a bag of nuts dangling from the cherry blossom tree.

Light crept through the clouds and Julia Finn could see a great sun, like a ball of fire, rise slowly over the chimney tops. The newly fallen snow looked red and glowing.

Then, suddenly, a black shadow darkened the back yard. The birds screeched. A huge cat swooped from the wall on to the tree, catching one of the little birds. The cat struck at it with its claws again and again until the lovely feathered creature stopped breathing and lay perfectly still.

Julia quickly unbolted the back door and ran out. But it was too late. She shooed the cat away angrily and bent down to pick up the dead bird. The snow was all around her, but she didn't notice. She crouched in her bare feet and saw that it was a little robin. He was still warm and she held him in the palm of her hand.

'Poor little thing, poor little thing,' she said, over and over.

And suddenly Julia Finn knew exactly what the something terrible was that she had felt was going to happen. Her husband would never come back. He was gone and he had taken his secret with him. She knew she must stop waiting for him. And thinking this, she began to cry.

A spot of blood from the robin's chest fell on the snow and she carried him over to the tree. Then she dug a hole and buried the little bird there, at the edge of the bulging roots. A wind blew and a few withered leaves fell on the ground from the branches overhead.

Julia Finn went back inside, locked the door and climbed the stairs to bed. This time she knew she would fall sleep. But just before she closed her eyes, she made a decision.

'When my baby is born, I will move far, far away. It

will be just me and my child and we will be strong together.' Then she pulled the blankets up to her chin, gave a deep sigh and fell fast asleep.

The snow fell for several more days and Timothy's father never came home.

A week later, Timothy was born on Christmas Day and a week after that, just as she had said, his mum bought Boat Cottage in Rowanstown, by the sea.

❋   ❋   ❋

Timothy tried to imagine it was just a story like all the ones Julia told him before he fell asleep – but this one was different because it was real.

When she had finished, he said, 'But will he ever come back?'

Julia sighed. 'But we're doing fine, aren't we? Don't worry about it, Timothy. Maybe some day ...'

Her voice sounded weak, and Timothy had a sinking feeling that Julia was telling a half-truth, the way he often did when he had a problem with one of his stories.

'Can I go out to play now?' Timothy needed to think about it all on his own. Julia nodded. She needed some time on her own too.

'We did love each other, Timothy, you know. He was so excited about having you. But he was sad. He was troubled. We ... well, we fought sometimes. We didn't always get on.' For a moment she heard the plate smash, the door bang again. 'It was something he had to sort out himself.'

'But will he come back?' Timothy shouted, and, not waiting for an answer, he roared: 'He's mean to leave us! He'll never come back!' And he ran out of the studio and up the stairs, banging the front door behind him.

Left alone, Julia stared at the package thrown on the floor. The handwriting frightened her. How could it be? she thought. How could her husband have sent this present to her son after what had happened so long ago? How could it be possible? She sat down on the sofa. Feeling a cold air pass over her, she pulled a cardigan around her shoulders.

＊　＊　＊

The sea air bit at his skin like a wild animal. Timothy raced from the hill down to the pier's edge without stopping for a breath. Gregory and all the fishermen were at home with their families and their boats looked shabby and forlorn, bobbing close to the harbour wall.

Timothy called out to his friends the gulls. Surely they'd make him feel better? But when the great black-backed birds swooped down over the waves, Timothy was shocked that all he could hear was a high-pitched cry falling from their beaks. He threw stones into the rough waves, hoping the sleek-headed seal would bob up to talk to him. But when he did appear, he showed no interest in Timothy, just gave a deep groan and flipped back into the sea quickly.

Something was changing. Is it possible, Timothy thought, that I can no longer see and hear words in the special way I was able to? Is my magic slipping away?

He made his way back along the cliff path. A group of

sheep huddled against an old stone wall.

'It's my dad. I never really knew about him,' Timothy began to explain to his friends. They had always been such good listeners. But the sheep seemed afraid of him now and scuttled away over the fields towards a tiny shed filled with hay.

Maybe he shouldn't have expected to keep his gift all his life. Maybe losing it was part of getting older? But it was sad. He would miss his chats with all his friends. How he had loved listening to all their talk and seeing their words rise in the air like strange shapes.

Maybe he shouldn't have expected things always to stay the same. Maybe the mysterious silver notebook and all it meant was part of his growing up too?

Thinking these thoughts, Timothy slumped down at the side of the road. He could feel the present in his pocket and he pulled it out. The late afternoon sun made the silver cover dazzle and Julia's pen fell from between its pages and on to his knees. The two gifts looked so bright, so silver.

He thought of the words his father had written.

To arrive where we started ...

It was then that Timothy began to write. The words flowed from the pen on to the beautiful yellow pages and, somehow, they made him feel calmer.

Things were changing, but he knew what he loved. He would never stop loving his mother and maybe some day he would meet his father and love him too. And though he hadn't met him yet, he could at least imagine him, write stories about him in this dazzling, mysterious gift he had been sent on his eighth birthday.

Something was changing – but Timothy would never stop loving words too. He couldn't hear them magically as he did before, but he would write them down instead, make up his own special stories, create a new world for himself.

And, thinking this, Timothy felt better, and the words flowed from his pen.

Once upon a time, there was a man who left home a week before his son was born and never came back. He travelled far away but never once stopped thinking about his wife and child ...

Timothy wrote on and on until he heard his mother call out his name and knew it was time to go back. He stood up and made for home, his notebook and pen in his hand. The two presents, in the moonlight on Christmas night, shimmered side by side. Strange, Timothy thought, how well they fitted together.

Chapter 5

Rolling Down the Mountain

It was two years later and early summer. Timothy was heading up a winding path high up above the cottage – a path that he had never noticed before. For Rowanstown was a surprising place. Just when you thought you knew every part of it, another laneway or field would appear to have an adventure in. This is why Timothy loved it so much and would never dream of living anywhere else.

He could hear a herd of goats nearby, their neck bells tinkling in the morning air like little giggles.

Then, suddenly, just when he felt every muscle in his body was about to crack into tiny pieces and blow down to the sea below, he spotted what looked like a large stone, shaped like a bench, jutting out from the mountain. A perfect place to sit and write.

All morning an idea had been growing in Timothy's head and his fingers were itching to scribble it down. He had a story to finish and he thought he'd found the perfect way to end it.

His silver notebook was moving this way and that in his pocket as though it too knew that soon it would be filled with more magical words. Ever since Timothy had been sent it in the post he had never stopped writing in it, and in a strange way he felt every story brought him closer to his dad who had sent him the notebook.

'It's as if he knew I wanted to write. As if he knew I loved stories. But how could he? He's never even met me?'

Timothy edged his way on to the granite bench and opened his notebook. The yellow pages glowed in the winter sun and Julia's pen felt smooth to touch as he began to write.

He was writing a story called 'First Day at School'. Miss Cornellie had asked that every child do it for homework. Timothy decided to make up a story about an ordinary boy called Joe Jones who found himself going to an extraordinary school. He had already begun it and was dying to finish it.

As Joe walked down the lane with his dad, he saw three, four and then more chimneys come into view, rising higgledy-piggledy over the top of the hill ahead.

It was then Joe saw that the chimneys actually belonged to something – a huge, sprawling house with enormous windows glinting in the morning light. But, wait a minute! Joe had never seen such windows before.

'Look, Dad, rockets and stars, big trains in the windows!' He held his father's hand tight.

'And can you see that ship over there?' said his dad. 'Doesn't it look like it's moving? It's even better when you're inside! All the brainwave of Mrs Moriarty. Children love looking down at the sea from the other side of those wonderful windows. It makes school a happier place. Yes, it must be the best school in the whole world!' Joe's father said, his voice full of happiness. 'It's called Chimneys, you know.'

'Chimneys,' Joe whispered to himself. Then he heard a strange voice call out.

'Mr Jones! – what a joy,

to see you here with your little boy!'

Joe couldn't be sure, but did this lady's words nearly sing, as if they were full of music? He had never heard anyone speak like that before. But his dad didn't seem too bothered by it, so why should he be?

'Sorry we're a bit late for Joseph's first day,' he heard his father say.

'Oh really, Mr Jones, please don't worry.

There was, after all, no great hurry.

It looks like Joe's as bright as can be!

He'll love Chimneys, just wait and see!'

Joe beamed up at Mrs Moriarty. He liked her. Just then two faces, their tongues sticking out, popped up from a nearby bush. Joe's Dad and Mrs Moriarty had their backs turned and didn't notice, but it was Joe that the two little girls seemed to be teasing.

'Daddy's boy! Little wimp!' he heard them whisper. Their fingers poked at his side.

'Ouch!' Joe yelped, but his cry was drowned out by Mrs Moriarty calling.

'Nan and Nat, oh, where have they got to?

They knew they should have been here to greet you.'

Joe noticed that Mrs Moriarty's words sounded annoyed and the twins came running towards her, twigs still caught in their hair.

'Your daughters, I presume?' Mr Jones was smiling.

He mustn't have noticed a thing, Joe thought, as he rubbed his side. He could feel a bruise beginning to spread across his skin from where the twins had pinched him. They were right on top of him now and he could see that they certainly didn't look kind like their mother, Mrs Moriarty.

Slugs! Joe thought. Their mouths are like creeping, horrible slugs! I don't think I like these two very much! No wonder their mum sounds cross when she sees them coming!

Mrs Moriarty held her hand out to Joe.

'Come with me, right this way!

I'm sure you'll enjoy your very first day!'

From that moment on, everything happened so fast that Joe hadn't time to be afraid.

His dad left him with Mrs Moriarty and headed off down the mountain path. Turning to watch him go, Joe chuckled to see that Dad had been in such a hurry getting him to school that he had forgotten to dress himself properly. Joe saw his dad's dressing gown flutter in the wind and noticed how bright his red pyjamas looked in the distance. How funny that Mrs Moriarty hadn't noticed!

But the twins hadn't missed it.

'Your Dad's a weirdo!' he heard the twins hiss together. 'Aren't you ashamed that he dresses like that?'

Shouldn't Mrs Moriarty scold them for speaking this way? But she didn't seem to hear them. She had other things on her mind. She must find a class for Joe.

Timothy liked the story so far, although it did make him feel a bit sad. He would love to be able to walk to school with his own dad, love to be able to chat with him and hold his hand – even laugh at him when he did silly things like wear his pyjamas outdoors!

He began to wonder what to write next when

suddenly an almighty noise reached him from above. But before he could turn around to see what it was, something came hurtling towards him – he felt a kick, a slap, saw dust rise all around him and then everything went dizzy inside his head as he fell, face down, into a prickly gorse bush. To protect himself he rolled forwards and then found he couldn't stop. Just what was happening Timothy wasn't sure, but he couldn't stop himself from rolling on and on, down the mountain.

Chapter 6

Fleur

It was as though the mountain with its gravelly path was pushing him further and further down towards the sea, towards Boat Cottage far below. On and on he rolled, clutching at twigs and stones. He couldn't stop. At last a huge bush on a broad ledge brought him to a halt. For a second, he lay on his back with his eyes closed, trying to figure out exactly what had happened, when suddenly he heard somebody whisper into his ear – somebody with a slightly foreign accent.

He opened his eyes slowly to find someone staring down at him. It was a person with very short hair, dressed in dungarees and a T-shirt, with feet laced into scuffed trainers.

Timothy couldn't be sure if it was a boy or a girl.

Freckles dotted this stranger's nose and cheeks. Timothy leant up on one elbow and peered closer. He saw more – large blue eyes staring at him and a full, cheeky mouth opening into a wide smile.

Finally he realised it was a girl, about his own his age, looking back at him. Her cropped white hair fell jaggedly out from her head like petals, and Timothy was reminded of the bright flowers that lined the twisting lane up to Boat Cottage.

'Oh, *pardonnez moi*! I am so sorry. It was me who pushed you. But I didn't mean to. One of those horrible goats frightened me and I ran to get away from them and then tripped and then I hit you and you rolled and rolled and I did too ... oh *non*, I am so sorry.' She didn't sound very sorry. If anything, her voice sounded as if it was laughing.

Timothy now saw that she was also covered in dirt, just as he was from rolling half way down the mountain. I suppose it is sort of funny, Timothy thought, though part of him was still a little angry with this girl for tripping and sending him flying. And where was his notebook? He looked around frantically and saw it had landed right beside him. He was still clutching his pen in his right hand.

'Oh, it's okay.' Timothy decided it was best to be kind to this girl. After all, he didn't know her. He would wait and see what she was like before he made up his mind about her.

'I have a tissue if you want to clean your face,' Timothy offered.

'*Merci beaucoup*, thank you, but don't worry. I have this.' And the girl pulled from her pocket a piece of silk, which had red and blue dots and stripes on it.

'The colours of my country, you see,' she said, spitting on the cloth and rubbing her face vigorously. Then, looking up at him, she asked, 'Well?'

'Well, what?'

'Well, aren't you going to ask me which country I'm from? Aren't you curious about me? Don't you want to be my friend?'

There was something so straightforward, so likeable about her, with her mixed accent and quirky looks, that Timothy had to admit that, yes, he did want to know, did want to be her friend.

'Okay, go on ... tell me about yourself.'

And so, the girl began her story. It was as if she had tripped and rolled down the mountain on purpose so that she could meet Timothy and tell it to him.

❀   ❀   ❀

'From the moment I was born, my father knew what to call me.'

'What?' Timothy asked, peering at his feisty new friend through the spikes of his unruly fringe.

'Yes. Oh, I get it! You haven't guessed have you? I'm from France, you see. I grew up in Paris. But I have excellent English because of my mama.'

Talk about vain, Timothy thought, but he couldn't stop listening.

'She's Irish, my mother. But I've got a French name.

Bet you can't guess it. I'll give you a clue. It's French for "flower".'

Timothy couldn't speak a word of French and stared back blankly at her.

'It's Fleur, silly. My name is Fleur. Can't you see it?'

She pouted her lips and fluffed up her white hair with her fingers, so that her fresh face stared out at Timothy, as if through a screen of beautiful petals.

'Look. I'm pretty as a flower. Fleur. That's what Claude, my Dad, thought when he first saw me. He's French. My mama agreed – she agrees with everything my father says! He wanted to put me in films in Paris – that's what he does with my mama – they make films. They both think I'm *talented* and have a *face the camera loves*!' Fleur spoke the last sentence grandly, and very vainly.

The way she speaks, she could easily be an actress on a stage, Timothy thought.

'But me, an actress? I can't stand all that stuff. All those hot lights and too much make-up that they paste like paint on your skin. So, I decided to change!'

'What do you mean – change?' Timothy said.

'Well, don't you think it's dull to be an actress?' Fleur slanted her head to one side and Timothy could see how tiny flecks of yellow shot through her blue eyes.

'So, I decided to change my life – wear jeans, throw out all those girly dresses my mother insisted on buying in expensive Parisian boutiques. I make my own clothes now. Well, add to ones I buy, really.'

It was then that Timothy noticed how her dungarees had lots of little flowers painted on them and her T-shirt had ribbons stitched to it with swirling glitter glued on here and there. All, obviously, the colourful handiwork of Fleur herself. Timothy looked down at his own jeans and shirt and felt suddenly quite ordinary.

'And I had a brainwave!' Fleur was still chattering away. 'I asked could I come to Ireland and live with my grandfather here for a while.'

She paused briefly for breath, then continued. She

seemed to love talking as much as Timothy did writing.

'My mama is Irish. Oh, I told you that, didn't I? Anyway, she grew up here, but then met Claude and *fell in love*.' Fleur fluttered her eyes up to the tree above them at this point and tapped her fingers against her heart.

'Then she moved to Paris and had me a year later. She was delighted when I asked could I come here to live with Grandad. To tell you the truth, I know they love me, but they also love making their films and were probably relieved to get a break from me – as you have probably guessed, I can be a bit of a handful!' Fleur smirked, and Timothy wondered how such a pushy, non-stop talker could be so likeable.

He grinned back at her as she wiped her hands clean on the edge of her by now very dirty piece of silk. Later, Timothy would realise that this was something Fleur often did.

'It's my lucky cloth,' Fleur explained. 'My father gave it to me before I left. Anyway, I was in Ireland only a few times when I was very young. I needed to see it again. So, I checked it out on the internet. It looked so beautiful that I knew I had to come back.'

Timothy pulled a piece of grass from his sleeve. 'What's the internet?' he asked shyly, afraid that Fleur might think him stupid.

'You mean you don't know?' Fleur's face just looked like Timothy was telling a joke. 'Surely you have a computer at home?'

Timothy had seen computers, but knew that Julia would never approve of one in Boat Cottage. She loved to use notebooks to fill with her sketches, and if she wanted to contact someone she would simply write a letter and post it off. And Timothy, too, loved his unlined copybooks where he drew his pictures. Most especially, of course, he loved his silver notebook where he wrote his stories.

'It's a way of finding out things really quickly on the computer! You can find anything you need to know on the net!'

'Like a big encyclopaedia?' Timothy asked, and Fleur raised her eyebrows.

'Yes, something like that. Now, hurry! We have to go back, I promised Grandad I'd be home for tea.'

Then in a flash, Timothy felt himself being pulled by Fleur down the mountain again.

Breathless, he called out to her: 'But wait. This thing, the internet – does that mean I could find any word I wanted on it? Find out what everything means?' This thought made Timothy's face hot with excitement. He was imagining how important the internet might be for his stories.

'I can't see why not,' Fleur replied, then began to run on ahead. 'See you tomorrow at school.'

'School?' Timothy was perplexed.

'Yes, the village school. I'll be in Miss Cornellie's class. I start tomorrow. Don't you go there? It is the only one around, *non*?'

And off the strange girl ran, her silk handkerchief flapping from her pocket, her hair like a white flag blowing in the wind. In a second, she had disappeared.

Timothy couldn't help noticing how quiet the mountain had suddenly become.

Chapter 7

Films and a Lost Father

As he walked home to Boat Cottage that afternoon, Timothy quickly went over in his head all that Fleur had said. She had said so many things – but one in particular had struck a chord with him.

Timothy had always loved films. This wild girl that he had just met, with her pretty face and spiky white hair, had said that *she* could have been in the films her parents were making if she had wanted to. But she decided against it simply because the idea bored her! *Bored her*? How could that be? Surely it would be *exciting* to be in a film?

Timothy had been to the cinema many times in Rowanstown with Julia. It was a huge, freezing hall that was sometimes converted into a makeshift cinema. But the sagging seats, the draughts, the faded, smelly carpets all seemed unimportant as soon as the lights dimmed and the films rolled up before Timothy's eyes.

Mostly he saw old movies, the kind Julia had adored as a child. They were shown on rainy weekdays after school or on lazy Saturday or Sunday afternoons.

Mary Poppins, *Chitty Chitty Bang Bang*, *Charlie and the Chocolate Factory*, *The Sound of Music*, *The King and I* – these were Timothy's favourites.

Julia's face would glow with excitement, her eyes reliving her dreams as a little girl, her fingers tightening over her son's hand.

'Isn't this great?' she'd whisper, and Timothy, seeing his mother so happy, would reply, 'Yes, yes it is!'

❋   ❋   ❋

But there was one film that stayed in Timothy's memory much longer than the others: three children lived near a railway in an old house with their beautiful mother, who was very sad. Her husband had to go away because he was brave and stood up for what he believed in. The children had lots of exciting adventures, but for Timothy the best part of all was the end, when the eldest girl, standing on a smoke-filled platform, finally saw her father emerge from the haze, the old train hissing behind him.

Timothy felt that Julia was like the mother in the film, and, although she never admitted it, he sometimes sensed moments of great loneliness in her life.

'Timothy, love,' she would occasionally say, 'I think I need to be on my own for a while. Can you go and play outside?'

Then Timothy would kiss her forehead and race outside to climb the trees, or dig with his spade in the soft soil, looking for insects and unusual stones.

But one day he peeped back in through the studio window and saw his mother inside, a piece of charcoal in her hand, drawing furiously, the stereo playing loud, unhappy music, her face twisted into an ugly knot, tears wetting her cheeks.

When he came back just before dinner, there was

Julia smiling happily, her arms extended to her little son. 'Well, you've been busy!' she laughed at Timothy, his knees covered in mud, his arms scratched from branches he'd crawled through.

And it was as if he had imagined his mother's unhappiness.

Only later, when his mother was washing the dishes, did he feel brave enough to creep down into the studio and rummage through her stacks of papers. And there, to his horror, he found sheet after sheet of dark drawings hidden among her usually bright and happy pictures. All of them were vague pictures of someone – a man – but it was very difficult to make out the features exactly.

It was easy for Timothy to guess what was happening. Julia obviously missed her husband as much as Timothy did his father. For, although Timothy had not even been born when his father had left, he really wanted to meet him, to touch him, to laugh with him – and to see his mother happy.

He tried to find the face of his father in the black drawings, but could only make out an outline, a blurred impression of someone he couldn't be sure of, would not recognise if he were ever to meet him. And this thought frightened Timothy.

Somewhere in the world his father was living a life, walking down roads, going to work, sleeping at night. But what if Timothy had already passed him on a crowded street, sat beside him on a bus, or stood next to him in a shop? How was he to recognise him? But worst of all, what if he had already met him – talked to him even – but didn't know?

Could his father be Mr Peters in the post office? Is that why his mum's voice tightened every time she went there?

But how could he have such a thought, Timothy wondered. Mr Peters his father? Mr Peters was far too old for Julia, and anyway *he* looked nothing like him! Besides, he showed no special interest in Timothy and if he was his father, wouldn't he want to get to know to his son?

＊　＊　＊

Remembering all these things, Timothy decided to talk to his mum when he got home. Meeting Fleur had shaken him up a bit, made him want to ask a few questions about his dad.

He had just made it home to Boat Cottage when the rain started to pour down.

'Julia?'

Julia was sitting cosily by the fire in the studio, sipping hot chocolate, the raindrops beginning to patter on the window pane.

'Who is my dad, really? Where is he gone?'

'My goodness, only in the door and you're already asking me such difficult questions!' Julia half-laughed. But Timothy could see she was a little uncomfortable with his question. 'What's brought all this on?' she asked.

Timothy explained about the stone bench and how he was writing there when Fleur tripped and pushed him down the mountain. He told Julia all about his new friend and her mother and father and how it got him thinking about his own dad.

Julia listened and sighed and then took a long time to answer. She had always expected that her son would ask more questions. Since his eighth birthday, two years ago, he had said nothing about his father – had seemed more engrossed in writing his stories than anything else. She had hoped she would be prepared for it. But now words seemed useless.

'I know you tried to tell me all those years ago. But now, I want to know more. What was his name?' Timothy wasn't giving up. He *needed* to know more.

'Sounds like this Fleur girl really made quite an impression on you. She sounds very interesting, I'd love to meet her some time. But about your father … well, I named you after your dad.'

'Timothy? He's called Timothy too?' This bit of information had Timothy hopping with excitement.

'Yes. His name was Timothy too. But, Timothy, like I

said before ... he was sad before he left. I knew something was bothering him, something he had to do. And, you know what? Sometimes I think ... well, it sounds silly ...'

'Go on, Mum, what?'

'Well, I think sometimes that you have to leave the people you love most and search for just what might make you a better person.'

'And if he finds what he's looking for ...' Timothy's face glowed with hope, 'doesn't that mean that he might come looking for us then?'

'Oh Timothy, I can't promise you something like that. But what I want you to be sure of, is that your father was very excited about the idea of you being born, and I know he would love you if he were to meet you now.'

'Really?'

'Really.' Julia pulled her son close to her and tickled him. 'Really, truly, really, truly, really!' She was laughing now and so was Timothy, the air filling with their togetherness, embracing them like a warm blanket. But as Julia's face turned away from her son a coldness filled it, which, luckily, Timothy did not notice.

It was no wonder then, especially after this conversation with his mother, that Timothy could not watch the end of the film *The Railway Children* without dreaming that it was *his* father stepping out on to the smoky platform, the huge old train spluttering behind him, his arms outstretched to his son, running, running to him. Home at last! There would be whoops of joy, his father throwing him over his shoulder, his mother smiling at the station's gate, a delicious welcome dinner bubbling back at Boat Cottage, sweet cooking smells filling the air.

Chapter 8

The Next Day at School

The next day at school everyone crowded around the new girl, Fleur, intrigued by her strange clothes and funny accent. And when Fleur told Miss Cornellie that she already knew Timothy, they were put sitting together and were to remain the best of friends from then on.

But at lunch break, when Fleur began to boast about her father, the film-maker, Timothy remembered how she could be annoying sometimes and felt a story coming on to impress her.

'I have a brilliant dad too. He's an explorer and off on a huge adventure in Alaska now, looking for the Ullu-mullu Bear – a bear with five feet and green eyes and bright yellow fur that no-one has spotted yet! But my dad will. He's going to catch him and when he does, he's coming back to Rowanstown and we're going to have a huge party! And it'll be all over the ... the ... internet!'

'The net! Incredible!' Fleur was impressed. 'I would love to meet him!'

Timothy grinned. If his dad wasn't around, at least he could make up stories about him.

'My father, the explorer!' Timothy muttered to himself. 'I like the sound of that!'

❋   ❋   ❋

The bell rang and all the children lined up to go back into class. It was time to read out the stories they had written for homework, 'First Day at School'.

As it actually was Fleur's first day at this school, Miss Cornellie told her to just listen and enjoy what the others had written.

The children had all written about their own experiences of coming to Rowanstown National school for the first time. But when Timothy began to read his story out, it soon became clear that he was the only one who had written about an imaginary school and had tried to feel what it was like to be somebody else – a boy called Joe, going to a school called Chimneys.

Timothy's words rose clear through the classroom and everyone was soon hushed by the story. The boys and girls leant forward and looked as though they didn't want the story to end. How they would love to be Joe Jones and go to a school like Chimneys with its crazy windows and headmistress talking in rhyme.

Timothy had got to the part where Mrs Moriarty was searching for a class for Joe.

'The class for you is Number 3!

And the teacher is – Miss Bee!'

They were at the top of the house and Mrs Moriarty flung open a huge door. Inside, three steps led down into a long attic lined with desks and chairs. It was all bright as could be. Enormous sky-lights let the morning sun flood the room from up above. And the far wall was nearly all glass too – shaped like an open book with words cut deep into its pages.

Joe felt strange being so high up. How far below the world was. Pairs of bright nine-year-old eyes looked up at Joe as he came in. Then, across the room came a tall lady, her hair tied up in a bright yellow bun.

It looks like she has a beehive on her head, Joe thought. Her name, Miss Bee, really suits her.

'Welcome to your first day at Chimneys, Joseph,' she was saying. 'It's nearly lunchtime. Here, take a seat by the window. You might feel a bit strange there at first – we're so far up here – but after a while, you get used to the height. Isn't the view amazing?'

Everyone's desk was a different colour and Joe's was painted a bright blue. He slid into the seat Miss Bee was pointing at. Peering out the window, Joe felt suddenly dizzy. There was a drumming sound in his ears and his cheeks felt very hot. Joe felt like he was about to be sick.

But then, something strange happened ...

Timothy stopped for a second and looked at his friends. They all seemed to want to hear what would happen next. But there was no big ending to his story, just a quiet finish. Timothy was tired of reading stories that weren't about what people really felt like. Last night, he had stayed up late writing in his silver note-book trying to write how Joe might *really* have felt on his first day at this magical school called Chimneys. Sometimes stories can be about small things and still be good, Timothy decided, and so he finished Joe's story this way:

A lovely feeling rose from the pit of Joe's stom-ach. The whole classroom was welcoming him, making him feel safe. He didn't feel one bit afraid.

He thought of his dad going home, his pyjamas blowing in the breeze. Then he thought of the strange but amazing school his father had brought him to. And Joe suddenly felt proud of him. He had the best dad in the whole world!

Joe sat back into his chair. Were all first days at school like this? He wasn't sure. But he felt really happy.

'I like it here,' he whispered. 'I really, really like it!'

And turning to Miss Bee, Joe felt a slow smile creep across his face.

He would never forget his first day at Chimneys school.

Everyone clapped.

'My goodness! What a good story, Timothy Finn!' Miss Cornellie smiled at him.

'Now, everyone, I can see you all really enjoyed it too – but can anyone tell me what made this a good story?'

There was a silence, a shuffling of feet, then Marcus said, 'Well, I liked the way it wasn't just boring old Rowanstown school. It was a cool school! I'd love to go to Chimneys!'

'Yeah, I loved the magic windows and the way it had a funny headmistress,' Amy said.

Then Fleur's hand rose. 'Miss Cornellie? I liked it because ... you see it's my first day at school and so far it's been a really happy one. Timothy's story made me feel like Joe – like I sort of knew him.'

'Exactly,' Miss Cornellie beamed. 'In a way, that's what good stories do. They make you feel like you know the people in them – they bring you into a world that isn't your own, but one where you feel very much at home. This is just what Timothy's story does.'

Fleur winked at Timothy. 'Well done!' she whispered. 'Wish I could write like that!'

That's twice today I've impressed her, Timothy

thought, feeling all happy inside from Fleur's praise.

Timothy couldn't wait to get home to Boat Cottage and read the story to Julia. In his pocket, he felt the silver notebook grow warm and then twitch a little, as though delighted with the story inside.

Chapter 9

Through the Pantry Door

Fleur's grandad, it turned out, was Mr Peters, and Fleur lived in the house at the back of the post office.

Some weeks later, after school, Fleur and Timothy were in the pantry downstairs at the back of the post office. Shelves lined the walls. Each shelf was stacked with all sorts of jars and boxes, containers and food baskets, all labelled neatly and ordered alphabetically.

'Your grandad must be a very organised man,' Timothy said.

'Oh, all those labels were done by my granny. She's dead a few years now. She lived through the war when there was very little food, so she was always stocking up on things. That's why there's so much stuff here! My grandad just keeps the old system going – I think because it meant so much to granny.'

Almonds, anchovies, artichokes, asparagus, aubergines, avocados, bacon, bananas, basil, beans (cannellini, green, runner, white), beef, beetroot, bread, broths ... the words swirled in Timothy's head and even though he had just eaten lunch, he thought he heard his stomach rumble with a deep hunger.

How could he not be tempted to have a little nibble of something? He reached for a pile of iced cupcakes.

'Help yourself,' Fleur said. 'Grandad won't mind. He'll be delighted *someone* is eating the food. Now, look, I want to show you something.'

It was Timothy's first time in the house at the back of the post office and he didn't know what to expect. Fleur was unbolting a big, green, wooden door and suddenly the dark interior of the pantry gave way to colour and brightness. Fleur raced on ahead and Timothy, rubbing his eyes, stumbled after her. It was like coming out of a dark cave into light.

✳   ✳   ✳

The pantry door led out into a beautiful garden –
brighter, more sweet-smelling than anything Timothy
had ever been in before. And there, swaying on a swing
dangling from an old sycamore tree, was Fleur, smiling a
triumphant smile.

'Now, aren't you glad I invited you to my house?
Nobody else from school has ever been here,' she
laughed.

'So, I'm the lucky one, am I?'

'I suppose.' Fleur was pursing her lips together now,
licking them, so that they glistened. 'You don't make
such a bad friend after all. *Les enfants*, I mean the children in Miss Cornellie's class are nice but you ... you
have always seemed different to me. Ever since you
read that story on my first day at school.'

'Really?' Timothy suddenly felt embarrassed and
changed the subject. 'I never thought there was such a
big garden was at the back of Mr Peters's post office.'

'I know! All the work of my granny. I wish she was still here …'

Fleur was still speaking when there was a mad scramble from the far corner of the garden and Timothy suddenly found himself on the soft grass, a white, scraggy little dog jumping all over him, licking his face, nuzzling into his neck.

'Dog, come here!' Fleur shouted, but the dog seemed intent on rubbing himself against Timothy and ignored Fleur.

'What a funny dog. What's his name?'

'He doesn't have one,' Fleur scowled. 'I found him wandering the beach one day and Grandad said I could keep him until his owner turns up as long as I look after him properly.'

'But don't you call him anything at all?' Timothy was bewildered.

'Dog. Just plain old Dog. And I won't change it unless someone comes up with a better name.'

Timothy bent down and rubbed Dog's belly. As he

did so, he could feel his notebook press heavily against his thigh and pulled it out. The sun glistened on its silver cover and Fleur gasped loudly.

'What's that?' she wanted to know. 'It's so bright in the sun!'

'Oh, just something my dad sent me for my birthday on Christmas Day two years ago.' Timothy felt his voice swoop low, like an injured bird falling from the sky.

'Sent you?' Fleur never seemed to miss a trick. 'Was he away? I know he's a great explorer but doesn't he even get home for Christmas Day? My dad's always off filming but he'd never, *never* miss being with us for Christmas. *Mais non*! Where was he?'

'Look, do you really need to ask? I don't have to tell you everything, you know.' Timothy surprised himself by suddenly sounding angry. He really didn't feel like making up a big story for Fleur again about his father, the famous explorer.

'Okay, okay, don't get so tetchy!' Fleur moved away from Timothy and slumped close to a pile of lavender, plucking at the purple flowers and pressing them close to her nose. 'I love the smell of this stuff! It makes me feel so sleepy.'

She began to roll her sweatshirt into a pillow shape and then lay down, resting her head on it. Some of the ribbons she had stitched to it fell like colourful wisps of hair across her face. She stretched her arms backwards, clasping her hands under her head and gave out a big yawn. Fleur was not someone who held grudges against anyone for too long.

'Don't worry,' she smiled at Timothy now. 'We all have our secrets. Why should you tell me something you don't want to? Maybe another time?' and she closed her bright blue eyes, fell silent and went to sleep.

It was, Timothy thought, as though a great light had been suddenly sucked from the garden.

Dog shook himself, gave a deep sigh, then flopped on Timothy's knee, wagging his tail gently on the lawn, until gradually he too fell asleep.

✳ ✳ ✳

Left alone with no-one to talk to, Timothy began to do exactly what he had been doing ever since he had received in the post on his eighth birthday the mysterious gift from his father. He began to write.

And in doing so, he began to try again and again to make sense of his life so far, of the gift he once had, of the words he had lost, and of his father, whom he feared he might never meet in his whole life.

It's to do with words. I love them – I mean, really LOVE them. And what's strange is, the words – at least up until I was eight years old – seemed to love me too.

Since I was a baby I was able to see words. It was as if they fell out of people's lips like beautiful bubbles. That's if people were happy – but if they were angry or cross, I could see the words twist into the sky like ugly smoke. I know it sounds strange – but an even stranger thing was the fact that I could sometimes hear what people or animals were thinking, without them ever speaking. It was rare when that happened, but it was usually when I needed to know something important.

And then, when I was eight, everything changed. It all just seemed to disappear – the gift, I mean. And so, I began to use words in a new way. I began to write stories in this notebook my father sent me for Christmas that year, even though I've never met him because he left my mother just before I was born.

Timothy wrote on and on, the silver notebook glowing in the sun, as though filled with a powerful energy.

So, my beautiful notebook, you are where I write all my special thoughts. You are where I try to come closer to the magic words I lost, try to understand my life with my mum – and where I try to get closer to my father who went away.

How can you love someone you have never even known? And yet I do. I love him. Love my dad.

Timothy stopped writing and began to run his fingers along Dog's back.

And then Timothy did what most writers do. He began to softly read out loud the words he had just written, changing lines here and there, adding new sentences, listening to what he had written.

Fleur rolled on her side on the soft grass, her head turned away from Timothy, as though she were deep in sleep. But her eyes were open and she was listening to Timothy's words, her heart beating.

Love my dad. She felt tears tug at her eyes and suddenly missed home, missed her mama and Claude, her eccentric, loveable papa. She had believed Timothy's story about his dad until she checked out the Ullumullu Bear on the internet one day and discovered there was no such creature. She knew then he had made it up. And if he had made up the bear, then he had also made up the story about his father. But she had said nothing. Now Fleur was hearing the real story – a story she would never tell anyone because she knew it was Timothy's own secret.

Imagine never, ever even *meeting* your dad, Fleur thought, *c'est terrible*! And an enormous wave of sympathy for her new friend flooded her heart.

Then suddenly it was as if her own father was there with her again, and they were standing together in the Tuileries gardens, rain softly falling down on the sandy gravel paths, the majestic trees and the staring statues, the glass pyramid of the Louvre gallery glistening in the distance.

Her father was holding an umbrella over her head, though he himself was getting soaked. It was just a few days before she was to leave for her first year at school in

Rowanstown and her father was giving her advice.

'Try and see the best in people, Fleur. Try and believe in them. What you give to others you will get back many, many times over. And be kind to those in pain – you never know when you might be down, when you might need their love and help too.'

And here was Timothy Finn, a ten-year-old boy without a father, a boy who loved to write. Fleur felt her father's arms wrap around her, heard his advice in her head again, over and over like a spell.

She would be kind to Timothy. From now on he could trust her as someone who would never let him down. She would always be there for him. And maybe after a while he would stop missing his dad. Because from now on, Fleur decided, she would be Timothy's best friend. She rolled over on to her back and opened her eyes.

'Oh, have I been asleep for long?' she asked innocently.

'Just a little while.'

Fleur heard Timothy quickly close his notebook and

put it in his pocket again.

'What have you been up to?' she asked.

'Oh, nothing, just writing a bit. I didn't wake you, did I?' Timothy asked, fear racing like a shadow across his face. 'It's just I sometimes read out loud what I've written, to understand it better.'

'Oh no. I heard nothing. I was fast asleep,' Fleur said and beamed her beautiful wide smile at Timothy.

Then they both jumped up and began to run around, laughing with delight at having such a quiet, beautiful garden to play in.

Dog yelped and leapt close to their heels and Timothy thought he would never forget this day.

And after a while, when they grew thirsty, they sipped the cool water from the garden tap and crunched apples from the orchard at the end, its trees heavy with bright green and red fruit.

'I suppose we'd better go back inside. We've homework to do,' Fleur said at last and patted Dog. 'Don't worry, old fellow, I'll be back out later,' and she pulled a bag from her pocket and poured dry food into a bowl. 'Grandad doesn't really like him indoors but sometimes I do sneak him in to sleep on my bed.'

Dog whined with delight and immediately began to munch and crunch his way through his dinner, swinging his tail back and forth happily.

Then Timothy and Fleur walked back across the grass, each lost in their own thoughts.

I love Dog, Fleur was thinking.

So much to write about, Timothy thought.

❋   ❋   ❋

When Timothy went home to Boat Cottage that afternoon Julia's face was bright with expectation, wanting to hear about Timothy's visit to his friend's house.

And though he told his mum all about the garden and Dog and the beautiful things he saw, Timothy never once spoke about what he had written in his notebook there while Fleur was asleep. Something Fleur had said was right. Everyone has secrets. Maybe, some day, he would tell his mother what he spent most of his time thinking and writing about. But not now. Not just yet.

Timothy smiled up at her. 'Mum! What's for tea?' he asked.

'Oh Timothy!' she laughed. 'How can you always be so hungry?'

Chapter 10

Baked Brains

Fleur never told the whole truth. She didn't lie exactly, she was just careful not to reveal too much about herself. For instance, it was quite a while after meeting Fleur before Timothy even knew where she lived.

Then one day Fleur took him to the pantry and the garden and introduced Timothy to Dog and everything changed. It was as if she had wanted to feel very comfortable with Timothy, to trust him, before she let him in to her world. And now that she had, Timothy often went to play with her in the garden at the back of the post office. But he had never been upstairs to see where she actually lived.

Then one afternoon, Julia sent Timothy on an errand to buy some stamps.

'How are you, young Timothy?' Mr Peters asked, 'And your mother? I saw her out by the rocks sketching the other day. My, but she is dedicated to her art, isn't she?'

'Yes. She loves her work,' Timothy replied, hoping Mr Peters wouldn't start asking too many nosey questions, as was his habit. All Timothy wanted was some stamps and maybe to see Fleur if she was around.

Through the back door behind the shop counter, leading into Mr Peters's house, Timothy suddenly saw a flash of white hair. Then a body dressed in a striped top and denim dungarees sped by and up the stairs. Fleur. What was she waving at him frantically for?

Oh, thought Timothy, I'd better go and find out what's going on.

The cash register was ringing up the total when Timothy looked up at Mr Peters and innocently asked, 'Would you mind if I went up to say hello to Fleur?'

'Of course not. She should be finished her study now. Here's your change. Do you know the way? Through the hall and up the stairs. You can't miss her door upstairs. You'll see why!' And Mr Peters rolled his eyes in amusement.

Timothy went in under the counter and through the hall, which acted also as a long, shelved storeroom stacked high with envelopes, boxes of stamps, pens, sellotape and a huge pile of notebooks that made Timothy want to reach out and touch them.

Part of him was jealous of Fleur for living in a place that sold notebooks and pens and for a few minutes he forgot about going to look for his friend. He had just taken a dark blue copybook in his hand and was wondering how much Mr Peters would charge for it, but then he put it down and almost reluctantly went upstairs. Immediately he heard a familiar sound coming from one of the rooms. It was a noise he had often heard before, in Miss Cornellie's class or in the post-office garden. It was a sound made by somebody blowing into their mouth, pursing their lips outwards and gurgling.

It was the noise Fleur made when she was

concentrating hard. It was a habit she had developed when she was a little girl. Some children suck their thumbs. Fleur liked making bubbles inside her mouth.

Following the sound, Timothy quietly walked down the corridor. Mr Peters's floors were covered in soft carpet. Nobody could hear him. In Boat Cottage it would be a different matter. Julia had taken great pleasure in pulling off all the musty carpets there and polishing the original floors beneath. She loved their gleaming look, not minding that every single step or movement sounded on the creaking boards. You could never enter Boat Cottage without being heard.

Timothy was standing now before a bright red door with *Do not come in! Privat!* hung on a sign dangling from the door knob.

The gurgling, blowing sound was getting stronger and stronger. Timothy was not afraid. It was only Fleur, after all. But then a terrible thought came to him. Maybe he had got it completely wrong. Maybe it was another person inside. Someone he had never met before. Then what would he do if caught by a complete stranger creeping around Mr Peters's house?

He was about to turn on his heel when suddenly the door burst open.

'I knew it was you! You're such a sneak, Timothy Finn, creeping around! Oh well, now you're here, you may as well come in to my room. I don't mind. That's why I was waving at you. I wanted you to come up. Grandad was annoyed with me for having Dog stay here last night and he told me to go and read some school books but I was bored. Then I saw you coming in.'

'It's *private*,' Timothy, half-listening, teased. 'The sign. You've spelt it wrong. P-r-i-v-a-t-e.'

Fleur raised her eyes to heaven. Always the clever one, her face seemed to say, and she shrugged her shoulders at him.

✳   ✳   ✳

Fleur's room was a large space that ran the width of the back of the post office. A huge circular window looked out over the rambling garden below and Rowanstown's church spire was visible in the distance.

'So, this is where you live. Amazing!' Timothy said.

'Yes. My Granny loved living here so much. My grandparents moved here after my mama left for France. They felt they needed a change from living in the city where my mama grew up with them. The sea air suited them here.'

'And the best part is,' she continued, with a sweep of her hand around the room, 'they made this room into a little flat for my mama whenever she came to visit with me as a baby and my Dad. After Granny died, my parents' work got very busy, though, and they don't come to visit much these days. So, I thought sending me here might keep Grandad company.'

It was then Timothy noticed the little alcove with the kitchen counter-top, the cooker and fridge, the door leading into a small bathroom.

'Grandad doesn't have to worry much about me here,' Fleur said, watching Timothy's roving eye. 'I'm completely independent. I can even make my own food. Want some?'

Timothy never could say no to food and Fleur knew it. She was soon pouring something into a saucepan, turning the knob on the electric cooker.

'You see, Grandad gets busy in the post office. So, I look after myself mostly. And I love cooking, just like my mama. Grandad's often said I can have friends over but I know he's tired after work. Anyway, I don't really like to be disturbed after school. Grandad respects my wishes.' It was Fleur-The-Little-Princess speaking now, Timothy realised. 'You sit down,' she ordered. 'Dinner will soon be served.' There was a stirring sound, a clink, a scraping and then a plate appeared. What a strange display of food, Timothy thought.

But Fleur looked delighted with herself. 'Baked Brains! You'd better eat quick or I'll gobble them all up! Yum!' she said, reaching for one of the weird shapes in front of Timothy.

Fantastic names for food. Julia and Fleur would get

on well, Timothy thought. Still, he felt a little nervous. Were these really brains? He wasn't sure he should eat them.

Fleur popped one in her mouth. Timothy gingerly followed her and began to nibble carefully at one of the 'brains'. He couldn't believe it! They were delicious.

'It's pastry rolled into a shape like a brain – I saw a real brain in a science museum once in Paris. That's how I got the idea. And it's stuffed with peanut butter and has heated marshmallow sauce on top. *Superbe, non*?'

'My mum would love this. Marshmallows are her favourite treats. You must make these in Boat Cottage for her some day.'

Pretty soon, Fleur and Timothy had eaten up all the Baked Brains. Then, sitting on the soft window seat, feeling all full of marshmallow and peanut butter, the two friends began to talk.

Chapter 11

The Photograph

'I found something here the other day, by accident,' Fleur said. 'I must show it to you.'

Fleur opened the window seat and tugged at a large, dusty album, grunting loudly. Timothy helped her lift it on to the cushions and knelt down to open it. *A Photographic History of Rowanstown* was typed on the inside of the album. And scrawled beneath it were the words *Compiled by Sebastian J. Peters*.

'Wow!' Timothy said, staring at black and white photographs of the town in the 1890s.

A moustached man wearing a pin-striped apron stood below a shop sign: *Morrissey's and Sons, Victuallers*, it read. Barefoot children in petticoats and puffed, knee-high trousers, played with hoops on the streets. There was a blur of carriages and horses speeding by in the background. In another photograph, a man in top hat and tails, his hand pushing a watch and chain into his pocket, briskly crossed a street. His wife, wearing a long, dark skirt and high-necked blouse, followed behind, a poodle on a lead beside her.

Timothy could make out Rowanstown's main street and most of the main landmarks. The central park, with its neat borders and rose bushes, hadn't changed much and the weather cock, still there on the top of the Town Hall, could be seen clearly in one photograph.

'It was obviously a project Grandad began, collecting old photos, but it seems to stop in the 1970s.'

Fleur was flicking forward now and Timothy could see a flash of modern life, coloured photos, women in mini-skirts, cars, sunny family holidays.

'But where would he have got them all?' Timothy asked.

'I don't know. Stuck in second-hand books, markets maybe. I know he used to go to house sales when old things were being sold. Maybe he found some there,' Fleur said. 'Now, this is what I wanted to show you. Take a good look.'

At first Timothy didn't quite understand why Fleur found this photograph so interesting.

It showed a girl – she looked about ten years old – standing in front of a painting. She was smiling broadly and holding a sign. *First Prize*, it read.

This was obviously why she looked so delighted. Her picture had been chosen by the judges as the best in the competition.

She wore a bright blue pinafore, black shiny shoes and knee-high white socks – the clothes looking dated, old fashioned. A red ribbon was tied to the side of her hair. A group of grown-ups all around her were clapping and two boys – the only other children in the photograph – beamed with delight at their friend's success.

Behind the gathering, Timothy could make out the huge, oval, stained-glass windows of the Town Hall.

'Look. It's the hall in Rowanstown! Is that it? Is that

what you wanted to show me?' Timothy was excited now.

'No, you dummy! Look closer! I can't believe you're not getting it!' Fleur half-laughed, half-scoffed at her friend.

What was it about this photograph? Timothy leaned closer, studying every detail.

Then the girl's dark hair and full face, her bright eyes and lively smile suddenly became familiar to him.

'Julia!' he whispered. 'It's my mum. But ...' he rubbed his hand across his forehead as if a fever were starting there.

'She was here as a child. Didn't she ever tell you?' Fleur had turned investigator now. 'It's possible she may have only been here for a short time. But isn't entering a painting competition something you do in a place where you live, not somewhere you're just passing through?'

'Maybe ...' Timothy was perplexed. He had always thought Julia kept no secrets from him. Why hadn't she told him? Is that why she decided to come to

Rowanstown after he was born? Because she had lived here as a child?

The afternoon seemed suddenly different.

'Can I take the photo home?' Timothy asked. 'I think I'll show it to Julia … see what she says. She was a great painter even then, wasn't she?' He began to smile at Fleur now.

But why didn't she tell him about living here? Oh well, everybody's allowed to have secrets, Timothy thought. Hadn't he decided not to tell Julia about what he wrote in his silver notebook? But still, it was strange …

Then something moved in his memory. What was it Miss Cornellie had said on his first day at school about Julia? She had known her when she was young. Had Miss Cornellie lived here too as a little girl? Timothy wondered. Might his teacher have been somewhere in that hall all those years ago when the photograph was taken of his mum receiving the prize?

'I think I'll head off now,' Timothy said. 'Thanks for the delicious food. See you at school tomorrow.'

Outside he began to race down the road with the photograph tucked carefully in his jacket pocket.

'Oh Timothy,' Fleur whispered after him, 'you've missed the most important thing.'

❋   ❋   ❋

Julia was pleased to see her son home. She laughed when she heard about Fleur's recipe for Baked Brains and said it sounded delicious. Of course they could make it some time together.

As she pottered about the kitchen, putting plates away and cleaning the counter top, Timothy could no longer keep his discovery to himself.

'Mum, why are you in this?' He held the photograph between them like an accusation.

Julia took the photo from Timothy and studied it closely.

'Oh my goodness! How funny! I'd completely for-gotten about this! I was so thrilled to have won that prize! Where did you get it?' Julia laughed.

So, Timothy explained about Mr Peters's album and all the old photographs.

'He must have found it in the Town Hall's archives. There was a local photographer there that day,' Julia said.

'But, Mum, did you live here in Rowanstown, all those years ago?'

'Well, yes, sort of. My parents would bring us down here for holidays – I spent most of my summers here. It was such a wonderful place to come to as a child. That's why I thought of it as a place for you to grow up in. I've always felt happy here.'

'But why didn't you tell me?' Timothy said.

'Oh Timothy!' Julia laughed, ruffling his hair. 'Don't look so worried. You never asked, that's all!'

And Timothy suddenly felt foolish for causing such a fuss and laughed too.

'Come on! Let's you and I go for a walk – go get some fresh air! You look far too pale today!' Julia reached for her coat and opened the back door.

Outside, the sea gleamed below like a gorgeous jewel and the afternoon was suddenly all theirs.

✻   ✻   ✻

Only later that evening, after Julia had wished her son good night, did Timothy pull the photograph out from under his pillow and look at it closely again.

There was something not quite right about it. Apart from Julia being in it, there was something else strange about the picture.

Then it was as if a very bright light was shining in the dark room. The clothes and hair-cut were old-fashioned, but the face, the eyes, the smile were the same.

Timothy was looking at one of the two boys clapping for Julia. The boy on the right of his friend. The boy with the green eyes and freckles and the rich, reddish hair. The boy who looked skinny for his age, but fit and happy. It was then Timothy realised that he was looking at himself. Or, at least, somebody, all those years ago, who looked just the way Timothy did now.

An idea, big as the world, floated through Timothy's mind. It had been a busy day, too much had happened and Timothy tried hard to push aside this idea. Better to leave things as they are, he thought. Better not to question things too much. I don't want to get hurt any more, he told himself over and over.

And thinking this, he opened his notebook and stuck the photograph under the back flap of the silver cover.

Then sleep came, like a comfort-blanket, soothing Timothy into a peaceful world for a while.

But a dream grew and grew in the night. The boy in the photograph became a grown man with red hair and green eyes – a man who ran towards Timothy and Timothy to him.

And one word blew twice from Timothy's mouth – twice across the grass to the approaching man, his arms outstretched.

Dad. Dad.

Chapter 12

The Magic Coat

Timothy was reading a story to the class.

On Ellie's tenth birthday a parcel arrived covered in stamps and tied with thick white string. It was from her gran – and that meant it would be very special!

Ellie loved her gran. Gran often told Ellie that she knew lots of secret tricks. But when Ellie asked what they were, Gran just winked and said, 'Well, now, they wouldn't be secret if I told you, would they?' and her wise old eyes filled with laughter.

Ellie couldn't wait to open the present. But she didn't have to wait for very long as the parcel gave a little jump and then burst open all by itself. A magic gift, Ellie thought to herself, and watched, wide-eyed, as something green and glowing, something soft and covered in silver sequins hopped out of the brown paper and stood all by itself in front of Ellie.

Ellie could hardly believe it. The most amazing coat she had ever seen was standing before her in her bedroom and now was moving towards her, its sleeves waving, as though trying to draw Ellie's attention to something in the left pocket. It was then that she saw the note, scribbled in Gran's big writing.

'Enjoy this coat as much as I have. But remember! It must be back by midnight – or else!'

Or else what? Ellie thought. But before she had time to worry about Gran's warning, Ellie felt the coat wrap itself around her. Suddenly the coat began to shudder and twitch. It twisted and turned, pulling Ellie this way and that. Hurry on, it seemed to say, there's no time to waste!

And then the most amazing thing happened. Ellie felt the coat lift her off the carpet, up over the bed and wardrobe. Somehow the window opened and somehow Ellie found herself flying through the air, up over her back garden and then high above the street where she lived. Below, she could see people she knew, chatting and laughing together.

'Hey! Look at me!' Ellie called out. But nobody looked up. How strange, Ellie thought, can't they see me? She swooped down by the school where her big brother was coming home, dirty and tired from football practice. Surely William will think this is amazing, Ellie thought, his little sister flying in a magic coat?

'Bill! Isn't this fantastic?' she came right up to his face, the coat flapping in the breeze, and shouted so loudly that she expected her brother to jump.

But he didn't seem bothered by Ellie's flying trick at all – in fact, he walked right by her.

It was then Ellie realised that not only was she flying in a strange and magical coat, but she was also invisible.

And thinking this thought, a huge feeling of freedom swept through her mind. If nobody can see me then I can do what I like and nobody will know what I'm up to at all!

And so, for the rest of that afternoon and well into the evening, Ellie had the time of her life – well, nearly!

Max, the amazing artist, lived down the road in a rambling old house. He usually painted all through the day and into the night. On the rare occasions that he did appear in his paint-stained dungarees, he looked pale-faced and interesting, like someone who has just woken from a wild dream. Ellie loved to paint too and always wondered what it must be like inside Max's house.

The coat seemed to know her thoughts exactly and suddenly Ellie was flying above Max's head in an enormous room, paint cans and paper everywhere, a huge easel facing the window.

The coat swooped down and within seconds Ellie was grabbing the brush from the surprised Max and painting on the canvas just where he was working. At first, he couldn't believe what was happening – a brush flying through the air, splashing paint everywhere, swirling this way and that. Then he became so angry that Ellie dropped the brush and made for the door, the coat trembling, as though afraid too.

'My painting! What's going on? It's being destroyed!' Max's eyes looked fierce and he shook his fist. 'I'm not afraid of ghosts! Whoever you are, get out of my home now! You're not welcome here!'

The whole house seemed to shake and Ellie felt the coat drag her out on to the street and high over several garden walls until she came to rest, panting, on Mrs Burke's apple tree. She had always wanted to eat those apples but every time she and William had tried to climb over the orchard wall, the old lady would race out of her house shouting: 'How dare you trespass on my property! Off with you both, young scoundrels!'

Now that I am invisible in this coat, Ellie gloated, I can eat as many apples as I like! It was fun to feel so free.

She began to devour the juicy apples, one after another, throwing the butts down on to the high grass below. And when Mrs Burke appeared, Ellie giggled to see her face go pale at the sight of apples falling, not whole but eaten, from her tree's heavy branches!

'Ha! That'll teach her not to be so mean to us!'

Ellie said to herself, surprised at how nasty she sounded. This coat was making her feel and do such very strange things that she wasn't sure if she was in control of her actions any more.

After a while, completely stuffed, Ellie felt the sides of the coat pinch at her as though to say, Let's move on! and they were off again, making more mischief.

Ellie and the coat flapped into a cinema and watched a whole film without having to pay – and nobody noticed. Later, she flew up and down the supermarket aisles, the coat's arms knocking packages off shelves, much to the alarm of the manager who stood so still in shock that Ellie thought he had become a statue.

Then, as though exhausted from all its adventures, the coat flew Ellie across the sea to a wonderful, sunny island where she lay in its warm embrace, like a giant soft rug in the sand.

Night came and Ellie was flying back over her home town again, feeling suddenly guilty about all the damage she had caused that day. Was Max's painting really ruined? Mrs Burke had a weak heart, she remembered, and she hoped she hadn't frightened her too much.

Ellie's tummy began to ache from worry and all the apples she had eaten earlier on. A nausea rose to her mouth and she thought she might be sick. It serves me right! Ellie thought, not sure if she liked the trouble the coat had got her into.

The coat, as though sensing her displeasure, began to shudder just as the cathedral clock below her began to chime. A terrible thought rushed through Ellie's brain. Midnight! She'd better get home! Gran said she had to bring the coat back by then, or else!

Or else! Or else! The words began to pound in Ellie's head like a bad headache. The night was suddenly freezing and to her horror Ellie felt the coat free itself from around her body. It was escaping, leaving Ellie to fall, fall, down towards the houses below, the twisting roads and lit-up cars. A whoosh – and the coat was free, flying up, up, where it disappeared behind a cloud and never came back.

'Help me!' Ellie tried to call out, but the wind took her words and swallowed them up.

Ellie fell down, down, down and then all went white.

Sunlight shone across her face and Ellie realised that she was waking up in her own room, in her own house. It was the next day. It must have been a dream. But then she saw the brown paper parcel all torn beside the bed and her gran's note flung there. But there was no sign of the coat.

Could it really have happened? Ellie wondered, a creepy sensation coming over her.

Downstairs, she heard the phone ring and her

mum talking to someone, then calling up to her: 'Ellie! Time to get up, you'll be late for school! It's Gran. She wants to know did you like the present.'

Ellie raced down the stairs. 'Gran? The coat ... I don't know where it is. I know you said you wanted it back, or else ... but ... it's gone!'

'Oh don't worry, dear! I only wanted it back to have some fun of my own! Young girls shouldn't be flying around after midnight, so I made it come home to me. I've been having a great time flying here and there well into the early hours! I'm only just back! Poor coat! It's exhausted. I hope you could control it, though. It has a mind of its own, that coat!'

'That's for sure!' Ellie said, not wanting to disappoint Gran, but relieved the coat was gone. 'There was never a dull moment from the second I put it on! In fact, that coat was definitely the most unusual birthday present I have ever been given!'

'But, somehow, I don't think you'll be wanting it again.' Gran said and Ellie heard her chuckle as she put down the phone.

✻   ✻   ✻

There was silence in the class when the story was finished and, for a moment, Timothy felt what all writers must feel when they read their new story out loud for the first time to an audience. Maybe they don't like it, he thought. Maybe I was a fool to think it was any good.

Timothy kept his head down and began to doodle on his notebook with his pencil. He knew he had based Ellie's present of the coat on his own present of the silver notebook. And because Julia was a painter, he knew well how Max would have reacted if somebody started to mess with his work. It seemed to Timothy much easier to write about things you had experienced yourself in some way. But maybe he had been wrong.

All these thoughts ran through Timothy's head just after he finished reading, his heart racing as he waited for the class to respond to his story. Then suddenly there was a loud clap and everyone was murmuring as though really delighted with what they had heard.

'Because this story is so full of imagination and so well written, I want to give this week's prize of Best Creative Writing Piece to Timothy Finn,' Miss Cornellie said, beaming at Timothy, who had gone a deep red.

'Now, children,' Miss Cornellie continued, 'Timothy's story got me thinking about the power of the imagination. If you have imagination, you can do pretty much any-thing you like in this life. And tonight, for homework, I want you to write a short review of your favourite book. The best way to feed the imagination is to read. Read. Read. Read. You're never alone when you have a book close by.

'Some of us are born readers. Some of us are born writers. And some of us are lucky enough to be born both.'

Miss Cornellie beamed at Timothy just as his silver notebook seemed to leap in his pocket.

'Writer,' Timothy whispered. *Writer*. The word grew in his mouth like a wish and a warm sensation flooded through him.

Chapter 13

The Mystery of the
Missing Writer

Fleur lost no time after school. She grabbed Timothy's arm.

'Meet me in the garden,' she said. 'I've something to show you.'

When Timothy got there after dropping his schoolbag at home and telling Julia where he was going, Fleur was bursting with excitement.

Dog, too, was wild with delight at having the two of them in the garden to play with. Fleur took a large carrot out of her pocket and threw it to Dog. He leapt far across the green grass and settled down to munch away beside the rose beds, the carrot held firmly between his paws.

'That'll keep him quiet for a while. Now, we can look at this in peace.'

She was unwrapping the piece of paper and Timothy could see that it was a newspaper article with a photograph of a man on it – a man he couldn't stop looking at – with large eyes that stared out of the page with a wild intelligence. Who was he? The man was leaning forward and behind his broad shoulders Timothy could make out row upon row of books. Between his fingers a fountain pen dangled.

'This is the writer I want to base my review on for class.' Fleur was triumphant. 'And there's no way anyone else will have heard of him, let alone have read him.'

'Why? What makes him so special?' Timothy tried his best to sound nonchalant but couldn't help being intrigued by the picture of this powerful man with his piercing look.

'Here, read this,' Fleur thrust the paper into Timothy's hands. 'It explains it all.'

was splashed in large dark letters across the front of the page.

The mystery of the children's author who has disappeared.

Below it, the story continued.

Ten years ago, Philip Montgomerie was being hailed as the most brilliant storyteller for children in the world. His novel, *Climbing Mount Ergo*, an imaginative tale of one boy's journey in search of a lost manuscript, delighted children and adults alike.

Film rights to the book were sold for millions and Montgomerie's career as a writer looked set to be the most successful of any living writer ever recorded.

But then everything changed. Philip Montgomerie disappeared. Nobody – his friends, his publisher, his agent – knew where he had gone. Just like the boy in his book – who, once he had found the ancient manuscript immediately threw it away – Philip Montgomerie seemed to have no interest in fame once he had acquired it.

So, the question is, where is he now? Is he hiding

away somewhere writing a sequel to his book – or has he by now finished several new novels that will thrill readers all over the world again once published? Or has the art of writing left him altogether?

Whatever the answer is to the mystery of this missing writer, one thing is certain: Philip Montgomerie's book *Climbing Mount Ergo*, will always remain in this reviewer's mind as one of the best novels ever written. And, for that, readers all over the world and for generations to come will be forever grateful.

Timothy lay back on the soft grass and let the newspaper slip from his fingers. A soft wind was blowing and in the distance he could make out a row of dahlias shake their crimson heads at him. Dog came over, licking his lips, a trail of orange from the carrot lining his mouth. He licked Tim's wrist and then curled up at his feet.

'Well?' Fleur's voice broke his mood. 'What do you think?'

'Incredible,' Timothy said. 'Some story. Where did you find this article?'

'My father posted it to me a week ago. He found the information about Montgomerie on some international books website. He's like that. Always looking for a new story for a film or a documentary he wants to make. And then a contact he knew sent him this newspaper cutting.'

'And does he want to make a film about this writer who's gone missing?' Timothy asked.

'Yes, I think so. But look, I don't care much about Claude and his films. What I do care about is this.' Fleur handed Timothy a tiny piece of paper.

'Tall Trees Manor, Blueberry Lane, Rowanstown', it read.

'Yes, it's true.' Fleur jumped around Timothy, laughing at the excitement of it all. 'Imagine! He lives near here. Philip Montgomerie lives in a house near here. But nobody knows that – it's quite secret, his house. Can you believe it? Claude had some really cool detective guy seek him out and he came up with this address. Isn't it amazing? Of course, my Dad wants me to find him and when I've done that, he's going to appear with all his film crew and make his documentary. But that's not the plan I have.'

'What do you mean?' Timothy could feel another Fleur plan coming on and his stomach tightened with fear.

'Well, look, as two children we stand a really good chance of getting this writer to talk to us and maybe even become our friend. The last thing Philip Montgomerie would want then is for the two of us to betray him by leading a film crew to him. He doesn't sound like a man who likes publicity, after all.'

'I suppose so.' Timothy could see sense in what Fleur was saying. 'But why do you want to meet him at all? Don't you think he should just be left in peace? And won't your Dad be annoyed if you find the writer but never tell him?'

'Oh, silly Timothy,' Fleur sighed. 'I don't want to find him for Claude, or even for myself. I want to find him for *you*.'

'For me?'

'Yes, you.' Fleur raised her eyes to the sky. 'Didn't

you hear Miss Cornellie? You're a writer. You have a *gift*, Timothy. You can write and you love doing it. I've seen how happy you are when you're scribbling away in your notebook. Don't you think meeting a real writer will help you to become better and better at it yourself? Who knows, you might even become the next Philip Montgomerie.'

'But ... but ...' Timothy knew it was useless arguing with Fleur once she got an idea in her head. And anyway, he liked the idea of one day becoming a real writer, liked that Fleur believed in him. He had never met a real live author before and the thought filled him with a sudden tingling feeling.

'All right. Let's go.' Timothy stood up and shook the grass from his clothes.

'Go where?' It was Fleur's turn now to be surprised.

'Let's go find this Philip Montgomerie at Tall Trees Manor – wherever that is,' Timothy said. 'And, fingers crossed, he'll be pleased to see us.'

Chapter 14

In Search of
Philip Montgomerie

Timothy jumped.

Down, way down from the top of the garden wall, away from the Post Office, away from Rowanstown, away on an adventure, his arms wide like a seagull's wings, his hair flapping in the wind.

He could get used to this – being brave and doing things he would never have had the courage to do before – he thought, as he grabbed at the ivy on the wall and held on, perfectly balanced, until he could decide what to do next.

Fleur was already ahead of him, Dog held closely to her tummy, as she made her way down, her deft movements making it clear that she had done this before.

'See you at the bottom!' she called up, and then disappeared under a clump of green.

Timothy was surprised to see that beyond the garden it was all countryside with no houses around.

'Here! Come here!' Fleur's voice was hushed but urgent. 'This way, quick! In case we get spotted! Nobody must see where we're going.'

The path was narrow and twisting as Timothy scrambled after his friend, Dog, now free, bounding along at Fleur's heels. Behind, the shape of the Post Office faded quickly. Timothy knew he would have to trust Fleur now and believe in what she had told him. Mr Montgomerie's house was apparently beyond the deep, enormous wood to which he could see the path led. According to Fleur the people of Rowanstown loved the sea too much to ever venture into this wood. They found it too dark and creepy. Some of the villagers even thought it was haunted and kept themselves and their children well away from it. Timothy could only hope that they were wrong.

They were entering the wood now and Timothy was conscious of soft twigs and moss underfoot and a smell of animals and trees.

Timothy stared anxiously around. The bushes seemed to be watching his every move. The trees became suddenly awesome. And from deep in the heart of the countryside, a cruel wind began to blow.

The wind tugged at his sleeves, burrowed its way into his chest and sent a noise like droning bees into his ears.

In the distance he could see Fleur and Dog begin to climb over a high gate. Timothy had no choice but to follow.

'Wait for me, Fleur!' he called, but his words were swallowed up by the howling wind.

✻   ✻   ✻

When Timothy caught up at last, Fleur was waiting by a huge beech tree.

'It's creepy here,' said Timothy. 'We'll never find the house.'

'Of course we will. My Dad sent me this map, so I think I know which way. Come on! We've left Rowanstown far behind now. We can only go forward. We have to find Philip Montgomerie.' She beamed at Timothy, and Dog pressed close to him, licking his hand, encouraging him too.

And before Timothy could reply, Fleur was linking arms with him and pulling him along. Then he noticed that every now and then her hand reached into her pocket and she took out bright beads and threw them on the ground behind them.

'What are you doing?' Timothy asked.

'Oh just a fairytale trick! They are from one of the necklaces my mother bought me! I never wear them, so I'm going to drop them along the path. Then we can find our way back.'

Timothy looked back. The beads shone on the ground and relief, like a warm, comforting drink, spread through his body. At least if he did get separated from Fleur and Dog, he would be able to find his way home.

* * *

Deep into the dark wood they went, the beads like a trail of magic breadcrumbs behind them. A badger snuffled in the musty bushes, but Dog did not react, so intent was he in moving with his friends to their journey's end. His brown eyes pierced the darkness like sparkling marbles. His ears stood upright, his tail wagging vertically.

Then, suddenly, there was an opening in the wood and it was as if a million bright beads lit the path ahead. Looking closer, Timothy saw that a path, covered in white gravel, lay before them. The path twisted through a line of tall yew trees. They must be the trees the manor is named after, Timothy thought.

And there in the distance stood the house, its four large windows glinting in the afternoon light.

'Walk on the grass in case we're heard!' Fleur ordered, back in her bossy mode again, and Timothy found himself doing what she said.

The tall grass was damp and high and wet his trousers

up to his knees as he waded through the garden towards the house.

It wasn't an especially large house, but the yews gave its driveway a grand appearance and the wide windows and elegant door, with its handsome porch, added to its noble look. It was a house that made Timothy think of cosy evenings by a fire and delicious home-made dinners.

Dog was now hidden completely from sight by the tall grass and Fleur picked him up, holding him under her arm. He seemed perfectly content with that.

And this is the way they crept towards the house of Philip Montgomerie, the missing, mysterious writer. One boy, a girl and a dog, not knowing quite what was ahead of them but wanting, all three of them, to get there.

❈   ❈   ❈

But then something unexpected happened. The sky cracked in half and there was such a tremendous rumbling that Dog leapt from Fleur's arm and made for the house as quickly as he could.

Rain fell in huge sheets and within seconds Fleur and Timothy were drenched to the bone.

'Quick! Follow Dog!' Timothy took control and raced after the little white creature, Fleur panting close behind.

'He can't stand getting wet!' Fleur breathlessly explained. 'It makes his bones ache and his skin go all itchy!'

They scrambled towards one of the windows, finding Dog there, his paws reaching up to the sill, his nose pressed against the glass. Raindrops fell in little rivers down all of their faces and Timothy noticed how pale Fleur looked, her drenched hair clinging to her wide-eyed face. They all were shivering.

And inside, it was just as Timothy had imagined. A fire blazed in the high-ceilinged room and a plate filled with steaming food lay on a large wooden table. But the room was empty.

Then a creaking sound filled the air. The drawing room's old mahogany door opened and in came a man, a book in one hand, a huge mug in the other. He was peering at the pages and distractedly heading for the table, sipping at his drink.

It was the very same man that Timothy had seen in the photograph. Timothy saw again how his hair, full of thick auburn curls, fell to his shoulder. He was broad-shouldered, well built – he looked like someone who knew what he wanted, someone you would be afraid to have as an enemy, but lucky to have as a friend.

Timothy liked the look of Philip Montgomerie.

But how would he react to trespassers on his property? Suddenly their adventure didn't seem such a good idea, after all!

Philip Montgomerie was reading a book out loud. His voice was rich and deep, and for a second, Timothy closed his eyes, lulled into a dream by its sound.

Then Philip Montgomerie reached for an enormous teapot on the table, poured some tea into his mug, took a huge gulp and spluttered: 'Ah! Disgusting! Totally cold!'

And before Timothy, Fleur and Dog had time to move away, the writer had opened the huge sash window and with a whoosh flung the tea-leaves out.

'Yuck!' Fleur couldn't contain herself. Not only was she drenched from the rain – but now she was also covered in cold tea!

'Who's there?' Philip Montgomerie called out. His hands stretched wide across the window-sill, he looked down and saw three pairs of eyes staring up at him.

He stared back, and then he spoke.

Chapter 15

The Large and Heavy Thing

Philip Montgomerie didn't roar.

'Children?' he asked softly, as though speaking to the rain and wind and not to Timothy and Fleur.

'Children!' he said again, shaking his head slowly, not believing what he saw crouched under his window sill.

Timothy, drenched and shivering, felt certain that this strange man's deep voice was the saddest thing he had ever heard.

'It's so long since I've met a child. Years, years ago ...' his words trailed off and he went into a kind of trance, his fine face staring out into the night, his hair lit by the fading light.

It seemed an eternity for Fleur and Timothy, hunched underneath, trembling with cold and expectation, waiting for the man to speak again. Would they have to stay prisoners to his sadness all night?

Timothy wondered then what deep hurt had injured this man so much? For, even though he was only ten years old, Timothy knew that every bit of human pain had a reason behind it. He had seen his mother furiously drawing her dark, dark pictures in secret. And perhaps somewhere, far, far back in time, even before he was born, he remembered an overwhelming sensation of sadness, and thought now that he could see his mum, on a snowy night, cup a dead robin in her pale and trembling hands, tears glistening in her eyes.

❋   ❋   ❋

But Timothy would never ask this writer, someone he'd never seen before, why he seemed weighed down with such a heavy sorrow. He was, after all, a trespasser on this man's land and, added to that, he was with a girl growing grumpier by the minute and a little white dog who was scratching wildly, his pink skin irritated by the rain.

'Can't you just let us in?' Fleur, fed up of waiting, was speaking now and Timothy was pleased to hear her voice ring clear as a flute. Fleur was not one for indecision!

'We're cold and wet and *hungry*!' she continued, emphasising the last word strongly and nodding towards the table of food. 'And Dog needs to be dried off quickly. You have a lovely fire going there. Why not share it with us?'

Philip Montgomerie snapped out of his dream and looked down at Fleur. Clusters of tea leaves streaked her white hair and a huge stain of rain and tea was spreading across the front of her shirt like a disease.

Timothy knew he didn't look so great himself. His arms and face were smudged with green ivy markings from the journey to Tall Trees Manor. And streams of rainwater were racing down the insides of his legs, making squelching sounds in his trainers every time he moved.

But worse, every item of his clothing was clinging to

him like a horrible, damp, extra layer of skin.

'Little girl –' the writer said and a lightness had entered his voice so naturally that Timothy wondered had he imagined his sadness earlier on.

'Fleur. My name is Fleur and this is Timothy, my friend, and Dog and …' Fleur didn't seem at all afraid of this powerful man with his flashing green eyes and deep voice.

'Timothy. Fleur. Dog.' Philip Montgomerie rolled the names in his mouth like tasty boiled sweets.

But then it was as if something sour hit against his tongue and his words came spitting out.

'Little French girl!' he hissed. 'I do not run a hotel to feed and dry you off! So kindly take your soaking friend and that itching mongrel off my land! This is *my* home and I don't want any strangers here – most especially children!'

'But …' Fleur was pleading now, even trying to smile her sweet smile, the one she used when she wanted something. But it wasn't working.

'Do you hear me? Are you deaf? Clear off!'

Then something came thudding through the air – something large and dusty and very heavy – and hit Timothy on the side of his head.

Philip Montgomerie slammed his window shut and drew the heavy curtains.

✻   ✻   ✻

'Ouch!' Timothy rubbed his ear and felt like crying.

'That's right! Make lots of noise! He'll just come out and chase us away if you keep going the way you are! What's that anyway?' Fleur hissed.

It was then that Timothy noticed the large and heavy thing resting on his lap – the thing that had hurt his ear only seconds before. It was a book, covered in a soft green velvet, with gold words splashed across the front.

'What does it say? What's it about?' Fleur pulled at Timothy's sleeve.

'I don't know. It's too hard to see. What will we do?' Timothy asked.

But before Fleur could answer, they heard a grumble within the house.

'My book! Of all the things to throw at them! I need it back!' and then there was a shuffle as the mysterious writer could be heard making for the window again.

'Oh no! Quick! Let's run!' Timothy shouted, picking Dog up and pushing Fleur back down the gravel drive as fast as he could, searching for the shining stones in amongst the trees that would guide them home, back to safety, back to the Post Office, back to Boat Cottage.

And under his other arm Timothy felt the huge, stolen book weigh heavily like a secret soon to be revealed.

❄   ❄   ❄

It was a relief to be back in the garden. The sun was shining there and everything seemed peaceful. It was as if they'd never left it.

Fleur had just finished eating a very large strawberry and was now busy making a daisy chain.

'You read the book, Tim,' she was saying. 'I'm too

tired. Then you can tell me all about it.'

Timothy had never stolen anything before and now here he was with a famous writer's notebook at his feet. He stared at the cover.

'Novel Two: Working Copy,' he read, 'by Philip Montgomerie.' There was a date – obviously when the novel was first begun – scrawled below the title in ink.

This book was started ten years ago and still isn't finished, Timothy realised. Maybe that's why Philip Montgomerie's voice sounds so sad. He just isn't able to finish his book.

And so, Timothy began to read, hearing all the time the great writer's voice sounding deep and strong in his head, giving the words on the page a rhythm, a life, a meaning.

And slowly Timothy came to realise that the story he had between his hands was a most extraordinary thing. Here was a real writer who loved words and knew how to use them. The sentences were magical, rich with ideas that kept Timothy busy turning page after page, his mind gobbling up the tale as though it were a delicious meal he just couldn't stop eating.

And Timothy felt comfortable reading the book because it was a story he had heard before, a story he knew well.

✳   ✳   ✳

'What's it about?' Fleur was waking up and stretching her pale arms.

'Well, I don't know if you would understand ...' Timothy held the book close to his chest, unsure if he could share it with Fleur.

'What do you mean? Me, an imbecile? *Non*, *non*, *mon ami*. My friend, I'm not stupid!' Fleur leapt to her feet, defending herself.

'Oh no, I didn't mean that. Well, okay, I'll explain. The bit I've read so far is about a father who leaves the mother of his child-to-be, and heads off, travelling all over the world, finally settling in a small village by the sea. Meanwhile, the baby is born and it's a boy, but the father never sees him, ever. He spends his whole life wondering what his son is like and misses him terribly. It's a really sad story and …' Timothy wondered had he the courage to continue.

'And? And what?' Fleur bent her face close to Timothy's. 'Tim, if you don't tell me, I'll read it myself!'

'Well, it's just that it's not exactly my story but there are bits in it that sound so familiar. There's a piece where the mum is standing in a garden and it's snowing and she is thinking of her missing husband and a bird dies and she is holding it in her hand, knowing the father of her child will never come back again ...

'Fleur?' Timothy held his friend's hands tightly in his. 'Fleur, I'm frightened. The story … you see, I've heard it before – well, some of it, anyway, from Julia. It's *my story*. I'm sure of it.'

Fleur drew away from Timothy and gave a deep sigh. 'I think I know what you mean, now,' she said.

'How could Philip Montgomerie write this story? Unless …'

'Unless he is your dad,' Fleur whispered.

The two friends stared at the large, heavy book and wondered what to do next.

Chapter 16

Peering Through the Window

Timothy knew he had no choice. He had to go home to Boat Cottage. One person would explain it all to him – Julia. He had to talk to his mum. Surely she could help him make sense of it all.

Timothy began to race along the pavement, nearly knocking Gregory down.

'Steady there, boy,' the fisherman warned. 'There'll be no taking you out in my boat if you're not careful of other people.'

'Sorry, Gregory, I'm in a big hurry … have to get home …'

'Anything wrong, lad?' Gregory looked concerned – but Timothy was gone.

Timothy wanted to talk only to one person: Julia.

He ran up the hill towards Boat Cottage, his scarf flapping in the wind. Far out to sea the lighthouse stood white and tall and Timothy could just about make out the other fishermen's boats coming safely into harbour after a hard day's work.

Behind him now, Rowanstown village nestled below the mountains, its houses lining the beach front, others stretching back towards the green, rolling fields. And at the end of the twisting hill path that he was running along, Timothy could see his house as it always was, shaped like a boat, face out towards the waves. Boat Cottage. His beloved home, where he and Julia had spent such happy times.

Was it all to come to a terrible end? Timothy felt a shivering sensation race along his spine. In his schoolbag the weight of the stolen book pressed against his back, as if it was pushing him on to find out the truth – a truth that would change his life forever.

The thought of telling Julia what he'd found filled him with dread. Things would never be the same again.

***

Timothy reached Boat Cottage and was just about to walk into Julia's studio when he heard a voice he knew well talking to his mum inside.

'Please don't cry, Jules. Here, have my tissue. I know it's been so hard for you and you've been so brave. You know, I'll always be here to help you, don't you?'

Timothy crouched at the window and peered inside. There, standing in his mother's studio, was his teacher, Miss Cornellie. What was she doing there? He remembered again Miss Cornellie saying that she had known Julia years ago, when she was young. But if that was true, since Timothy had started at school his mum had never invited Miss Cornellie to Boat Cottage and Timothy had never seen the two women together acting like best friends, the way they were now.

He heard Julia give a loud sob.

One thing's for sure, Timothy thought, I can't upset mum further now by bringing up questions about Dad, not when she's crying so much. I'll have to wait until the time is right.

Through the window, he saw Miss Cornellie hug his mum, then squeeze her arm encouragingly.

'You'll be fine, Julia,' she said. 'And don't forget, ring me anytime you need to chat. You must have got such a shock seeing that writing.' Miss Cornellie shook her head. 'Why on earth did you keep it all to yourself until now? You should have told me ages ago! And poor Timothy. Though, Lord knows, he does love that note-book.'

Timothy gasped. They had been discussing the parcel that had been sent him on his eighth birthday! Two years ago. It had indeed upset his mum greatly.

'Thanks, Nellie. You really are a great pal. Maybe you're right. It's been two years, after all. I should ring him. I know he hides away where no-one can find him. But I will.' Julia sounded very determined.

Timothy gasped. Was she really going to try to find his Dad and ask him why he sent the notebook?

'Silly of me to keep getting upset,' Julie continued, 'especially when things are going so well – Timothy's settled at Rowanstown school and we have a lovely home here. In so many ways I've been blessed. Especially in the friends I have,' and she beamed at Miss Cornellie. Then the two of them disappeared up the stairs towards the main door.

When they had gone and Timothy could hear Julia seeing his teacher off, he crept into the studio and up into the cooking cabin.

He hides away where no-one can find him … Timothy shivered. He had just heard his own mother admit it. Philip Montgomerie *must* be his father. A huge hunger overcame Timothy and he was just about to spread peanut butter on a thick chunk of bread when his mum appeared smiling at him, as if nothing had happened, as if it was just another ordinary day.

'Hello, my main man. I didn't hear you come in. How was school today?' she asked. 'Hey, I'm starving too. Make me a sandwich as well, will you?'

Then they both settled down to have a snack together, happy, as usual, in each other's company. There was no need to torture Julia with questions now. Timothy felt certain he had his answer, anyway. Philip Montgomerie was his father.

❋   ❋   ❋

That night, when he heard Julia settle down to sleep in her room next door, Timothy pulled the green book from beneath his pillow and switched a small torch on.

Alone, away from Dog and Fleur and the excitement of the day, Timothy became a real reader. Philip Montgomerie's words drew him into the story and Timothy gasped in parts at the beautiful way the language flowed. If only he could write like that.

He began to feel a great sympathy for the mother left to raise a child by herself, but also for the father who had left and was missing his boy terribly. Something – some awful truth – was stopping the dad from returning to his family and Timothy wanted to find out what that was.

But the story ended abruptly, almost as if Montgomerie himself was unsure of the reason, leaving Timothy feeling cheated, disappointed.

Timothy closed the book. This story was so like his own life that he suddenly realised how dangerous it was to have it here at Boat Cottage. How would Julia feel if she found it? She has been so upset today, Timothy thought, I mustn't let her see this.

Anyway, it was stolen property and he was sure Philip Montgomerie was anxious to get it back. If he really was his father, Timothy didn't want to have an argument with him before telling him he was his son.

Tomorrow, Timothy resolved, with or without Fleur, I'm going back to Tall Trees Manor and giving the green book back to its rightful owner. How I hope he is my dad!

Chapter 17

Becoming a Writer

Timothy didn't have to worry about Fleur. She wasn't at school the next day.

'Her grandad rang. She's got 'flu,' Miss Cornellie explained.

Timothy stared at his teacher. Should he mention that he had seen her through the window of the studio yesterday? Better not, he thought. If I do, she might tell Julia and then all my plans to visit Philip Montgomerie will be interfered with. And then I'll never find out the truth.

'You'll just have to survive without your friend today,' Miss Cornellie smiled, knowing how much Timothy and Fleur relished each other's company.

Timothy was relieved. Miss Cornellie didn't suspect anything and it wasbetter that Fleur wasn't in school. He felt that going back to Philip Montgomerie's house was something he had to do alone. If Philip truly was his father, Timothy wanted to be on his own with him to find out.

✳   ✳   ✳

After school Timothy sped down the street to the post office. Slipping through the side gate of the garden, he noticed that Fleur's curtains upstairs were drawn. She was obviously sick in her bed and wouldn't notice him in the garden.

Dog was delighted to see him and Timothy couldn't resist spending some time with the little white terrier, throwing a ball to him, playing chasing and finally, tickling his soft belly.

'You'll have to stay here this time, fellow. I can't bring you today. But I'll be back soon, though.' Timothy patted Dog, ruffling the white fur around his neck, and then he began to climb the old wall, searching for the ivy on the other side to bring him safely down into the countryside and on his way to the writer's house.

※　※　※

Tall Trees Manor was different today. The sun had dried up the puddles and the yew trees in the driveway looked more beautiful, less sinister. Flowers of all different colours lined the lawn and Philip Montgomerie's garden seemed almost as magical as the one Timothy had just left behind.

Timothy was suddenly filled with a burst of bravery and, raising his hand to the big brass handle, knocked boldly on the door.

It was only when he heard the sound of feet striding along the hall inside that he began to be afraid. What if Philip Montgomerie was as angry with him as he had been yesterday? A huge urge to run away gripped Timothy, but he held his ground.

'You've come this far, Timothy. Stay where you are,' he whispered to himself, watching the huge oak door swing open. 'This man is your father.'

What Timothy saw filled him with surprise. The

great, mysterious writer stood there, his huge shoulders filling the doorway, his auburn hair glinting in the light and he was doing something very strange. He was smiling.

Yes, an enormous grin was spread across his powerful face and Timothy, for a moment, was dazzled by the whiteness of Philip Montgomerie's teeth.

'I thought it was you. I saw you coming up the drive and couldn't help hoping you'd brought it. Did you? Are you here to give me my notebook back?'

'Of course. I have it here.' Timothy was amazed that words were coming out of his mouth, so in awe was he of the man standing in front of him. He seemed so different – more relaxed, happier. Had Timothy imagined the grumpy, roaring ogre that was Philip Montgomerie yesterday?

'Come in. Come in.' The writer flapped his great hands and directed Timothy into a vast hall filled with books, then down a corridor which led to a huge door.

Inside, Timothy found himself in the very room that

Fleur and he had been staring into yesterday. A blazing fire filled the room with a glorious heat and a soft sofa, piled with cushions, was drawn up close to it.

'Now, you sit and rest here,' Philip Montgomerie said, sighing loudly as he took the green book from Timothy's hands and placed it safely in a cupboard close by, carefully locking it with a key he had on a chain around his neck.

'You did the right thing bringing it home to me,' he said. 'I'll go make some tea.' And he disappeared out of the room leaving Timothy all alone.

Miss Cornellie always said that the best way to feed the imagination was to read and read. Philip Montgomerie must have an enormous imagination, Timothy thought, as he looked at the hundreds of books all around him.

Timothy began to wander from shelf to shelf, fingering the names of writers he had never heard of before, that he couldn't even pronounce – Chekhov, Dostoyevsky, Pasternak, Hemingway, Yeats and many more. Maybe when he was as old as Philip Montgomerie he would have read as much, know as much as him.

Then, moving back towards the sofa he saw on the table a book bent open, a pencil marking the page, as though Philip Montgomerie had been interrupted reading it by Timothy's arrival.

It was a poem – but no ordinary poem. The sight of it sent Timothy rummaging for his own silver notebook in his pocket. He opened it and read the inscription scrawled inside by his father.

> And the end of all our exploring
>
> will be to arrive where we started
>
> and know the place for the first time.

Then he looked at the lines in the poem that Philip Montgomerie had underlined heavily. There was also a great big tick beside them on the margin. They were the same lines as the ones in his silver notebook. Was it just a coincidence that Philip Montgomerie liked the very poem that his father did – or were they the same person?

Timothy felt a shadow creep over his shoulder and on

to the page and he jumped backwards, slamming the book of poems shut.

'I see you've been reading Mr Eliot.' Philip Montgomerie had a slight laugh in his voice as he balanced the tray on the table. 'Such beautiful lines. I often repeat them to myself out loud. They give me courage.'

'To do what?' Timothy asked.

'Why, to go on,' the writer said. 'Would you like some tea?' He began pouring the tea into two large mugs. 'Help yourself to some milk and sugar and chocolate biscuits,' he said.

Are you my father? Timothy wanted to ask, but instead he said, 'I'm sorry for what we did yesterday … creeping up your drive and running away with your book.'

'But you've redeemed yourself, young man. You brought back my precious notebook. That's all I care about. As I'm sure you know now from reading my story, I'm a writer.' He stopped and then asked, 'You have read it, haven't you?'

Timothy slowly nodded at him.

'As I expected,' the writer said. 'Well, no harm, I would have done the same. You're the first person to read it. That's really scary, you know. I've been afraid of anyone reading it for many years. I've been thinking about it all night. And, strangely, now it's happened it doesn't seem so bad.

'Look, let's begin at the beginning. Can we be friends?' He held out his big hand and Timothy found himself shaking it.

'I ... I only read it because ... because ... because ... well, Miss Cornellie, my teacher, says I can write and so does Fleur, my best friend you saw yesterday ... and I thought if I met you I might become a real writer ... and so I read your story to see what real writers write like ...'

'Goodness, what an outburst!' Philip Montgomerie was laughing again.

He flopped down on the sofa, cupping his mug between his hands and stared into the fire. The room grew quiet for what seemed like an age and then finally the writer spoke.

'So, you want to be a writer, do you?' Steam from the tea rose around his eyes like a magical mist. 'Well, I'm not exactly a perfect example of how to be one. I haven't even finished my book after years and years of trying to.'

'It doesn't matter,' Timothy said, 'it is the best thing I have ever read. I really wanted it to go on and on. Oh, please finish it. It's brilliant. I want to find out what happens.'

'Such praise. Thank you,' Philip said. 'And you? Have you written much?'

Timothy resisted the urge to show his strange new friend his silver notebook. Instead he pulled from his bag the story about Ellie and her granny's magic coat.

Philip Montgomerie folded out the copybook and began to read.

'Hmm.' The writer half-grunted when he had finished and then said. 'Yes, I like this – in fact, I more than like it! It's really very, very good! Well done. You know, when Ellie feels all free and happy when she wears the coat it reminds me of how I feel when I'm having a good day writing and all is going really well – when the magic of inspiration comes, just like a wonderful present! Were you pleased with the story?'

'Sort of,' Timothy said. 'But you know what? Sometimes I wish it was easier to write. I'd love to have a great flow with words like you have. Also, sometimes it seems so hard to get ideas about what to write. Do you find that?'

'Oh, all the time,' Philip Montgomerie replied. 'When a really great idea comes, that's inspiration. But most of the time it's hard work and waiting – waiting for the story to come together. Sometimes I think of writing as a curse – but then I know I would be very unhappy if someone was to say to me I could never write again.'

'I feel like that too,' Timothy agreed. 'It's just something I have to do – and I want to get better and better at it. That's why I thought I should meet you. I've never met a writer before.'

'Actually, you have,' Philip was smiling again.

'Have I?'

'Why yes, you silly boy. You! You've met yourself. And it seems to me if you keep writing and thinking the way you do, you're well on the way to becoming an even better writer than you already are.'

'A writer? You think I am one?' Timothy whispered and his heart swelled with pride. It had been worthwhile visiting Tall Trees Manor for this encouragement alone.

'You know what?' Philip said, 'I think I'm going to take the rest of the afternoon off and you and I are going to have an adventure. Sometimes it's great to write about something you've never written about before. Come on, let's go out and see what we can write about.'

❋　❋　❋

Leaving the library and fire behind, Timothy followed Philip down a back hallway, through a big, cosy kitchen with bright yellow walls and blue cupboards and then out a back door.

There Philip led the way up some granite steps, past a fountain and through a maze of green hedges, until they arrived at a circular green space with statues dotted all around.

'My Sculpture Garden,' Philip explained. 'Now, you pick a bench as far away from me as possible and choose a statue to write about. Look at it really closely. Try and imagine a whole story around what you see, and then in a while let's meet again and read to each other what we've written.'

'It's like an exercise at school,' Timothy said.

'Exactly. Writers often set themselves tasks like this to get ideas flowing. You'll be surprised what comes out. Now, good luck,' Philip said, wandering off, pen and paper in hand. 'By the way, that silver notebook I saw you with in the house will suit you fine for this bit of writing.'

He really doesn't miss a trick, Timothy thought. He must have seen my silver notebook when I was peering at the Eliot poem and he crept up behind me. Unless, of course, it was *he* who sent it to me ...

Timothy decided to sit cross-legged in front of a

statue of a young girl holding a bunch of flowers. He couldn't help noticing on the other side of the garden Philip's choice – a sculpture of a bearded man, stick in hand, dressed in a flowing tunic and cape.

Timothy thought a while, then began to write and write, only stopping now and then to read over what he'd written and to change a few things here and there.

When Philip called him over a while later, Timothy was amazed to discover that a whole two hours had gone by. He had been concentrating so hard, writing so fast, he hadn't noticed the time pass.

Then the fun began.

Philip read out his piece about a great king long ago who wanted to rule the world. And so, he left his wife and children and spent years fighting wars far away, all the time gaining control of more and more cities, until he had defeated all of his enemies and was crowned King of the Universe.

He returned home to his castle only to find his wife dead and his children all grown up and angry with him for having deserted them. They blamed him for their mother's death and would not forgive their father for his cruelty in leaving them.

It was then the king realised that for all his fighting and conquests he had gained nothing and lost the most important thing – the love of his family.

Timothy's story was about a little girl who brought happiness to everyone she knew. She was so kind that people began to think of her as a holy person. Crowds travelled from far and near to meet with her, hoping some of her goodness would rub off on them.

Then there came the coldest winter ever. The whole of the village froze. Animals died and people starved because they could grow no food in the ice and snow. They longed for spring, but it never came. Then the girl grew sick with pneumonia and everybody knew she would soon leave this earth. But she promised the people that when she died, flowers would appear on her bed and this would be a sign that the bitter weather would end.

And this is exactly what happened. She died just a

short while afterwards. And then, a wonderful thing happened: a hundred red roses appeared like magic on her bed and with them came the smell of spring. The sun came out, winter faded and the village was saved from any more hardship. The villagers built a statue of the girl holding a bunch of flowers so that every time they looked at it they would remember her goodness and how she had saved them.

Timothy and Philip listened to each other's stories and both agreed that they hadn't done badly at all.

'Writing every day helps,' Philip said, 'In fact, today has helped me a lot. Just remember, if you do get stuck, just pick something – anything – and you'll be surprised at how your imagination can begin to work.'

He was walking around the garden now and heading for the main door of the house.

'Will you come again?' he suddenly asked, surprising Timothy.

'Yes. I'd love to.' Timothy beamed back at him. Maybe they had become friends, after all.

'By the way,' Philip Montgomerie said, 'I forgot to ask. You know my name, but what's yours?'

'I'm Timothy – Timothy Finn.'

The great writer was silent for a while. 'Well, good-bye, Timothy,' he said finally. 'See you again sometime soon.' And he waved Timothy off.

That's the only thing, Timothy thought, turning to leave, his name is Philip, not Timothy. Didn't Julia say my Dad and I have the same name? Maybe Philip is just his writing name and his real name is Timothy?

* * *

Watching the boy run into the forest and head home, Philip went back inside to his library. There, he sat down by the fire, stoked the flames alive again and stared ahead, deep in thought, one hand drumming a beat on his knee.

At last, he spoke softly to himself.

'Well, well. Timothy Finn. Julia's son, I presume. At last I've met him, all grown up. At last.'

Chapter 18

In the Graveyard

Timothy and Fleur were lying in the long grass of the graveyard. All around them tombstones, dappled in green moss and dusty with spiders' webs, stood crooked like old teeth on the hill. The graveyard was on Rowanstown's island, joined to the village from the beach by a small, sandy slice of land.

When the tide was fully in, it was impossible to reach the island. But at low tide you could visit by simply walking along the beach and crossing the rocks which led to an old iron gate and steps going up to the graves.

There was an old abbey at the top of the island, looking out over the bay. It was deserted now, falling apart and filled with wild flowers and thick bushes. But Timothy loved to scramble through the ruin and peer out the arched, glassless windows at the view below. Far off, he could make out Boat Cottage, nestled in the cliff.

It was Saturday morning and Timothy and Fleur had just finished exploring the island. They lolled side by side in the morning sun, a half-finished picnic at their feet.

Below them, the sea was a foamy, bluey-green and shimmered in the light. In the sky an aeroplane was leaving a slow trail of white and Timothy wondered what it must be like to be so high up, looking so far down. He had never been in a plane. The marram grass whooshed in the breeze, sounding like expensive silk; the mountains nearby were full of glorious colours and Timothy thought how wonderful life could be.

He was just about to fall into a pleasant dream when he heard Fleur's voice beside him. She must have been talking all the time but he hadn't heard.

'... so you both wrote together in the garden, he gave you brilliant advice, even said you were a writer and then asked you to come again? Sounds like he liked you,

Timothy. He really liked you. When you become a famous writer you can thank *me* for finding Philip Montgomerie for you in the first place.'

'Yes, you were right. He was a great help to me and not at all the angry man we first met.'

'Do you still think he's your dad?' Fleur's eyes were filled with curiosity. 'Why didn't you just ask him?'

'Easy for you to say. You have a dad. I was afraid, I suppose, of what I'd find out.'

'And you haven't said a word to your mum either? Oh, Timothy. How do you ever expect to find out the truth?' A tiny ladybird was creeping through the spikes of Fleur's hair and Timothy brushed it away.

'I'm just not like you, Fleur. When I'm ready I'll try and find out.'

'Well, okay, Tim. But if a long time goes by and you've done nothing about it, I'll go to Tall Trees Manor myself and ask him – *and* I'll ask Julia.'

Timothy groaned at the thought. 'All right, all right. Now, can we change the subject?'

'I'd be delighted to. You can't imagine how *boring* it is for me always talking about you and your family. Come on, let's play hide and seek. You close your eyes and count to ten slowly while I hide.'

Fleur skipped away up the hill and Timothy turned his face towards the beach, counting in a dull, slow voice: 'One, two, three … four …'

Why am I always the one who has to search? Fleur always gets her own way, he was thinking. Next time, she can hunt for me and see how much fun that is. She usually hides in the abbey anyway, below the O'Grady tomb. I'll definitely find her there.

A great gull squawked overhead and Timothy stopped counting for a moment and let his eye rest on a gravestone he had never noticed before. An angel with the face of an innocent boy rested over the inscription and Timothy bent down near the grass, pushing it aside to see what the writing said.

There was a date.

Ten years ago, Timothy thought. The year I was born.

Somebody died the year I was born.

He pushed aside a piece of heather blocking the words and read further. Now he could see what it said.

❋ ❋ ❋

It was then the shaking started, followed by loud screeches that seemed to rise uncontrollably from the depths of his body.

And then, after what seemed like an age, Fleur was beside him, slapping his face and crying, 'Timothy, Timothy, what's wrong?'

Sobbing, he pointed to the gravestone.

Fleur saw the words and leapt back in alarm.

> In loving memory of Timothy Finn,
> aged 31 years

'What does this mean?' Fleur screamed. 'Are you a ghost? Are you already dead?' Her face had gone as white as Timothy's and she began to back away from him as though he frightened her.

'Fleur, don't be stupid. Don't you get it? I'm not dead. My dad is. That's my dad buried there. Philip Montgomerie and all that stuff … I was wrong. He's not my father. Ten years ago my dad must have died and been buried here.'

Timothy pulled the grass further back to reveal the rest of the inscription:

Will forever be missed
by his wife Julia
and son Timothy

'Oh Fleur,' Timothy said, 'this is awful. And look, there's that quote again', he pointed to the bottom of the stone, 'those lines from the poem – the lines he sent in my notebook. But wait a second …'

A thought so frightening was forming in his head that he could barely ask the question. When he did, his voice was low, troubled.

'How could my Dad have sent me that notebook for my eighth birthday if he was already dead?'

Fleur had stepped closer to Timothy again and was now squeezing his arm.

'Timothy this is getting too spooky. You'll have to go home now – quick! Hurry! Ask Julia what's going on. She's the one who'll know – and *make* her tell you. She has to. She's been keeping secrets from you for too long – and it's just not fair. Go on, I'll be fine. Just let me know what happens, okay?'

Timothy gulped and gave Fleur a quick hug. 'Thanks. You're right, I'll have to go home now. That's where the answer will be.' And he turned and made for the mainland, his heart beating strongly, a fever spreading across his forehead.

Left alone, Fleur roared after him, 'Good luck, Timothy, good luck!'

Then she turned her back on the gravestone, shivered a little and began to walk slowly down through the tall grass, home to the post office. Feeling lonely for her own mama and papa, she decided to ring them in Paris that night.

*　*　*

Timothy had never run so fast in his life. Over the dunes, down the dirt tracks, past Rosie's old collie dog barking in alarm at the racing boy. Through the village main street he ran, people stopping open-mouthed to stare at him.

'I didn't know Timothy Finn was such a good runner,' the butcher said to one of his customers.

'Yes,' the customer said. 'Have you heard the story about Timothy Finn? So tragic. She made us promise never to tell the boy. Looks like he may have found out something now, though.'

The butcher, having just recently moved to Rowanstown, leant closer over the countertop to hear the story about the boy and his missing father.

*　*　*

But Timothy, hearing none of this, ran on and on away from the village and out the cliff road until he came to Boat Cottage.

Julia was washing some paint brushes under the out-door tap, her dungarees on, a red scarf holding her hair back. She squinted in the sun at Timothy charging towards her, then dropped her brushes in alarm.

Chapter 19

Julia Explains Some Things

When Timothy grabbed his mum's hand and began dragging her down the path below the cottage and on to the beach, Julia thought at first it was some sort of game he was playing.

'Slow down, Timothy. I need to catch my breath,' she gasped.

But Timothy didn't say a word and continued to pull his mother along the sand towards the island.

'Where are we going?' Julia asked at last.

Then she saw the old graveyard up ahead, saw the determination on her son's face and a shadow crossed her beautiful face.

'But, Timothy …'

'No buts, Julia. This is something you need to explain

to me.' Timothy had never spoken so coldly to his mother before.

Julia's face paled. She pushed her son aside and sat down on the beach, her feet digging a hole, her toes squirming deeper and deeper into the damp sand.

'I'm not going any further, Tim, until you sit down too. You're right. It's time we talked. So, let's do it.'

Now it was her turn to be strong and Timothy wilted a little under her hard stare. He sat down, all his energy suddenly leaving him. To be faced with the truth at last was a daunting thing.

'The photograph you found in the post office,' Julia began, 'that really holds the whole story. Like I said, I came to Rowanstown often as a child – spent most of my summers here and loved it so much. It was here I began to paint, won my first art prize, made friends. But two of my friends were very special. Two boys. You saw them in the photograph.'

'One of them looked just like me … was that …'

'Your father? Well, yes. We became friends way

back then, grew up, met again in the city and knew we had always loved each other. We got married and everything was going to be perfect.' Julia's voice trembled. She bent her head away from Timothy and her words seemed to blow gently away with the sea breeze.

'But what happened, if everything was going so well?' Timothy wanted to know.

'I got pregnant in the first year of our marriage but your dad got very sick. It was cancer of the stomach and he was in great pain, but he never told me about it. He grew more and more cranky and I didn't understand what was wrong with him. We began to fight a lot. It was horrible. Later, of course, I knew why he left. Because …' Julia reached for tissues in her pocket and finding none there, pulled the red scarf from her hair and blew her nose in it. Timothy had never seen her do anything like that before.

'Then, Timothy, something extraordinary happened.' Julia's body began to shake as though a fierce storm was ripping through her. And her voice, Timothy thought, it sounds like a wild wind. But before he could watch what was happening more closely, his mother leapt up and began to race away from him along the sands, howling loudly, then sobbing, then whimpering, her hands clawing at the air, as though pushing demons away that were trying to lodge in her hair.

She was at the water's edge now, crying with all her heart.

He began to run towards her.

'Mum,' he roared. 'Julia!' At this moment he felt that his whole world depended on reaching his mother at the shore. And he was certain of one thing – he loved his mother more than anything or anyone else in the whole world.

Julia was kicking at the waves when he reached her, and sobbing loudly. Timothy had to wade into the sea to get close to her, the freezing water slapping its way through his clothes. He grabbed at his mother's waist and pulled her around to face him.

At first Julia stared at him as though he were a ghost,

then, as if waking from a bad dream and seeing how worried he was, her features softened slowly.

'Oh, Timothy. You've chased my demons away again, my beautiful boy.'

The pain was still there, in her voice, in the exhausted way she sighed, but now she took her son's hand and said 'Come on, let's go back up to the dunes where it's warm and talk some more.'

❋   ❋   ❋

Julia and Timothy lay in the sun.

'He left because he didn't want me to see him so ill. He left because he didn't want me to see him die. And because he didn't want me so upset just when I was about to have a baby.'

'But, Mum, you would have cared for him,' Timothy said.

'I know, love. Of course, I would. I would have *wanted* to look after him to the end. But he never even told me about his sickness, never contacted me after he left. I didn't know where he was. It was only later, when I read an article about people who are very sick that I understood a bit better why he did what he did. It was as if the illness had found its way into his mind too and turned him away from me and the new life that was to be you.'

'So, he ran as far away from you as he could.' Timothy was quiet for a few seconds, but then the questions came again, flooding his thoughts.

'But he's buried here, in the graveyard on the island. Why?'

Julia's eyes turned towards the Abbey and the headstones jutting up below it. She shivered.

'The other boy in the photograph was our great friend too. He lived near here. Your Dad hadn't seen him for years but found him again and went to hide away with him. He made our friend promise not to contact me. It was a pure coincidence that when you were born I moved here too. I suppose your dad and I always thought of it as the place where we felt most safe. I came here in my time of trouble and so did he,' Julia said, adding, 'but when we moved into Boat Cottage, I didn't realise that just a few miles away your dad was dying in secret.'

'So he did die ten years ago, the year I was born?'

'Oh yes, he did,' Julia said. She tugged at a bit of marram grass. 'But oh, how stupid I was back then. I made everyone here in Rowanstown promise not to mention your father to you, or that they had known the two of us as children, or that they knew of his death. Even your teacher, Miss Cornellie. Imagine! I swore her to secrecy too. I didn't even want you to know we were such good friends! But why shouldn't you have known? I was broken by too much grief, you see, and didn't want you broken too. I wasn't thinking properly at all.'

Timothy remembered for a second what he had seen that day he had peered through the window of Boat Cottage – his teacher comforting his mum. Things began to make more sense. He knew that when people were very sad they often behaved strangely.

'The only way I could think of to go forward was to

try and start all over again and be happy with you. And, so far, the villagers have always kept their promise – and my secret. And we have been happy, love, haven't we?'

'Of course we have, Mum,' agreed Timothy. 'But it was a mistake, Mum, wasn't it, to keep the truth from me?'

'It was, love, I know that now. But there's more to our story, Timothy. You see, just after we settled here in our new home my friend finally rang me. He couldn't keep your dad's secret any more. He felt I should see him before he died. I was shocked to hear he was so close by and hurried there, just in time. He was very weak but he did speak to me, said he was sorry for all the pain he'd caused by running away, said he loved me. He died with us right beside him and he was smiling ... at you.'

'Me?' Timothy felt as if a knife had been stuck in his heart. 'What do you mean?'

'Timothy, you did meet your Dad,' Julia explained slowly. 'I took you to my friend's house that day and your Dad died, happy to have met you at last.'

❊   ❊   ❊

A sandpiper pecked at the edge of the beach and the sea left trails of foam on the sand. The world was still going on as usual, but everything had changed for Timothy.

In all his thinking about his father he had never imagined such a story, never imagined that they had actually met. Now the thought that his father – the man he'd been named after – had actually seen him, had smiled at him just before he died, filled Timothy with a warm feeling.

But then the questions came back again, flooded through his mind and rushed out of his mouth.

'If my dad did die ten years ago, how come he sent me the silver notebook on my birthday? How come, Mum? It doesn't make sense.'

'Oh don't be angry with me, Timothy. Things got so mixed up after he died. I became so sad. I didn't want to see our friend again, felt he had let me down for not telling me immediately when your Dad went to live with him. And so, we didn't see each other for a long time.

Then, two years ago when you were eight, that parcel arrived. I was as surprised as you, Timothy. In fact, it frightened me. The name on the envelope was written in your father's writing. I was so scared. How could he send you a present if … if he was dead?'

Timothy and Julia both stared at each other and silence filled the air like fear.

'Then it dawned on me, of course.' Julia spoke now in a whisper. 'Someone else had kept the parcel and posted it to you years after your Dad had died and I began to guess who that might be.'

'Whoever it was must be very cruel,' said Timothy. 'That notebook made me worry and worry.' Timothy turned away from Julia. 'I kept thinking my dad might come back, kept wondering about the lines he wrote inside. It just made me miss him more.' Timothy began to cry and Julia pulled him close to her.

'I'm so sorry, Timothy,' she muttered into his neck, her tears mixing with her son's. 'So sorry, so sorry …'

Julia kept saying it over and over again and Timothy

too began to half-chant, 'It's okay, Julia, it's okay …' again and again, rubbing her face and hair, comforting her as she had always done for him in the past when he was hurt and needed her.

✳   ✳   ✳

At last, exhausted from the sadness, Timothy stood up and Julia thought for a minute that he was going to walk away from her.

Instead he turned to her and said, 'Mum, you're my best friend. But don't you think best friends should always tell each other the truth?'

Julia smiled through her tears. 'Yes,' she said. 'Yes, I do.'

They began to walk back towards Boat Cottage, arms linked, the graveyard far behind.

'Just one thing,' Timothy said. 'Did you figure out who sent the notebook?'

'Yes. He's a very private person. Someone whom your father trusted completely. Someone who followed your father's wishes and sent you the gift when you were old enough to appreciate it. Someone who has since become my friend again,' Julia replied.

'And what's his name?' Timothy asked, pushing the studio door open and walking towards the fire.

Julia looked at her son and said a name. It was a name he had heard before – a name that already meant so much to him.

Timothy sat down on the sofa, pulling some of Julia's sketches out from under his leg.

'I know that name,' he said. 'Mum, I've met your friend already. And he's my friend too.'

Now it was Julia's turn to sit down. 'He never said,' she whispered. Then she curled up in the huge wicker chair beside her easel and went silent for quite some time.

Finally she got up and went to the phone. And for the first time that afternoon, Timothy saw his mum smile.

In a few minutes she put the phone down. 'We'll be having a visitor soon,' she announced.

Chapter 20

The Visitor

When the doorbell finally rang, Timothy was ready for anything. The visitor coming down the stairs was heavy-footed, walked slowly and spoke softly to Julia. It was a voice Timothy knew all too well – so rich, so deep, so full of feeling.

But he didn't come into the studio. Instead, Julia took him out the side door, and Timothy could hear them outside on the deck, overlooking the sea.

Then the door opened and Timothy's mum came in. 'He'd like to talk to you on your own,' Julia said. 'Here, put your coat and scarf on. It's a chilly night.'

And so, Timothy Finn, all bundled up, went outside to meet Philip Montgomerie on his own.

✳ ✳ ✳

Philip Montgomerie was hunched over the balcony, his long, green coat rolling to the ground, his huge shape impressive in the dark.

When he turned, Timothy saw that his eyes were full of pain. Was it possible he felt as bad as Timothy did about the things that had happened?

'He was my best friend, Timothy,' he said. 'I only did what I thought was right. I never meant to hurt you. I just thought I should do what your father asked …'

The notebook jumped a little in Timothy's pocket and he pulled it out, its silver cover shimmering.

'I want you to have this back,' Timothy said. 'It was special to me because I thought it was from my dad who was alive and living somewhere else. It made me think he was coming back. But now I know you sent it. Now even the lines from the poem on the inside make me sad …'

'They were your dad's favourite lines,' Philip said.

'Even so, nothing is the same,' Timothy was downcast.

'Timothy, the notebook is special because of what's

in it – your stories. If you want to be a writer, you must keep it. God forbid – if I stopped you from writing I'd never forgive myself.'

Then Philip Montgomerie did something unusual.

The great writer came over to Timothy and knelt in front of him. He took Timothy's hands in his and looked up at the boy before him.

'You don't know how much your visit meant to me the other day. In the statue garden, writing together … it gave me energy … made me realise how important writing is, how much I want to do it. I was a fool to hide away for so long.'

Timothy thought of Tall Trees Manor and for a second was glad his father had found a safe resting place with his friend in that beautiful house.

'When Julia brought you to my house to see your father the day he died, I felt nothing but guilt. You were a beautiful baby boy and I had agreed to hide your father from you and your mother! But that afternoon, in my house, a great man died and Julia, for just a few hours, her little son in her arms, told me everything she felt. She told how devastated she had been by your dad leaving home just before you were born and of your coming here to set up home at Boat Cottage. After that, she couldn't bring herself to speak to me again – until recently.

'I knew there was a book there waiting to be written, imagining a different story – a story in which he went away, always longing for you and for Julia. I wanted to write the book as a way of asking your mother for forgiveness, and to take away some of her pain, I suppose, though I didn't realise that at the time. I began writing the very next day. But I struggled and struggled with the book for years, trying to find an ending. Then you came.' He looked at Timothy. 'You have given me the courage to finish it. And even if you never forgive me, Tim, I'll always be grateful to you for that. And if it is some consolation to Julia, that would be the greatest gift I could ever get.'

Timothy stared and stared at the writer. He had never

heard Philip speak for so long, or with such feeling and his heart warmed towards the kind man in front of him.

A moon shaped like a fingernail came out from behind a dark cloud and a ray of yellow light shone down on the wooden deck.

At last Timothy said: 'When I was a small boy, I seemed to hear words everywhere, even from the animals and birds. There was no end to them. But when I got a little older, I thought I was losing my gift. Then I tried to write, and I dreamed of becoming a writer one day. But you have made that dream real. I don't think I can give you the notebook back, after all. I'll need it from now on.' Timothy smiled at Philip and the great writer gave him an enormous hug.

'Friends?' Philip asked.

'Friends,' Timothy replied.

❈   ❈   ❈

Just then a loud shriek came up from the beach below.

'Hey, Timothy! It's me. Look who I've brought!'

Timothy peered through the dark and saw Fleur struggling along the sand, Dog at her heels. There was also a thin man in a smart suit following behind her.

'Can you believe it? My papa! He flew in to surprise me. He wants to meet Philip and make that documentary about him. Isn't it exciting?'

'A documentary? About me?' Philip Montgomerie went pale and began to shiver a little. He looked at the girl and her father getting nearer and nearer and Timothy thought he might run away any minute. Then he straightened up and took a deep breath.

'Well, Timothy,' he said, 'it's time I came back to the real world again and stopped hiding from everything. I think it would be very nice to have someone film me and ask me about my new book, don't you? Maybe not immediately... but sometime soon.'

'Of course, of course! That's brilliant!' Timothy clapped Philip on the back.

Down below on the beach Dog was barking loudly, delighted to see Timothy again.

Philip, Timothy and Julia could hear Fleur and Claude and Dog clatter up the steps to the deck. The night filled with laughter and greetings and shaking of hands. Fleur punched Timothy playfully in the stomach. Every now and then she would turn to wink or smile at her father and Timothy thought he had never seen her look so delighted with herself.

Dog fell upon Timothy, nuzzling his soft head into the boy's legs, snorting with delight, then rolling on his back for Tim to give him a belly-rub.

Everything is all right, after all, Timothy thought, tickling Dog's white hair. It was as if his life was suddenly one great, exciting story.

'Philip?' he asked. 'How will this story end?'

'As all good stories should, Timothy Finn,' Philip Montgomerie replied. 'Happily ever after.'

OTHER BOOKS FROM
THE O'BRIEN PRESS

A magical tale from a winner of
the prestigious Caldecott medal

'Gerstein's hybrid of fantasy and fable explores human nature, war, magic and music ... a vividly descriptive narrative with an unexpected ending.'
PUBLISHERS WEEKLY

Long ago when Gisella was a young girl in the Old Country, a land where magic still existed, she gazed too long into the eyes of a fox – and the fox stole her body. Trapped in the animal's body, with war raging all around her, Gisella had to find her family and try to get her own body back.

A compelling fantasy from an
award-winning author.

JOURNALS

A GREAT SERIES WITH WONDERFUL STORIES

First kisses, boyfriends, parents who don't understand, school, homework, friend trouble – sometimes there's just so much to deal with.

Every girl needs a journal.

THE LOUISE TRILOGY

Aubrey Flegg

WINGS OVER DELFT

As the daughter of a wealthy Dutch family, Louise Eeden knows that certain things are expected of her. When her father commissions a famous artist to paint her portrait, she reluctantly agrees. But lately things have started to move too fast in her life. Somehow everyone believes she is engaged to Reynier deVries; she is chaperoned and protected, a commodity to be exchanged in a marriage that will merge two respected pottery businesses.

In the studio with Master Haitink and his gangly apprentice, Pieter, Louise unexpectedly finds the freedom to be herself. But someone has been watching her every move, and her deepening friendship with Pieter has not gone unnoticed.

Raynier has spied on him, with the collusion of Louise's nanny, Annie, who hates Pieter because he is Catholic. Reynier's gang attack Pieter, leaving him badly beaten.

Defying everyone, Louise goes to Pieter's church to see for herself what Catholicism is all about, and she's surprised to find that it isn't as threatening as she has been told. Happy with her chosen young man, she walks with him in the countryside, and they have the first – and only – kiss. Fate has another surprise in store for Louise Eeden: in 1667 there was a huge explosion in Delft and from the artist's studio young Pieter looks in horror at the place where Louise's home used to be ...

THE RAINBOW BRIDGE

France, 1792. Revolution is sweeping the country. Eighteen-year-old Gaston Morteau leaves his village to join the Hussars of Auxerre, to the dismay of Colette, the young aristocrat whom his family has taken in following the deaths of her parents. Two years later, Gaston, now a lieutenant, rescues Master Haitink's portrait of Louise Eeden from a canal. From then on, Louise becomes his companion. She comes alive for him, as her artist creator had promised she would, sharing his experiences, witnessing the trauma of war, meeting Napoleon, and all the while probing his complex character.

When Gaston returns home on leave, bringing Louise's portrait with him, things have taken a disastrous turn. In order to prove himself a good *citoyen*, the Count du Bois has been parcelling off the vineyards on which the family depend, and the share to which they have rights has become too expensive to buy. Louise forces Gaston to give her portrait to the Count as payment and then finds herself embroiled in a tale of political intrigue and Gothic horror. When, finally, she is sold off to a Jewish trader her life takes a new turn ...

IN THE CLAWS OF THE EAGLE

Austria, 1913. Louise's portrait hangs in the home of the Abrahams family in Vienna. When young Izaac Abrahams develops as an infant violin prodigy, Louise is his audience and critic. Meanwhile, Erich Hoffman is growing up south of Vienna in a family dominated by a grandfather who plants the seeds of anti-Semitism in his mind.

Izaac is at the height of his career when the Anschluss takes place. He is sent to Terezin camp where he works with children on the opera *Brundibar*. Louise's portrait is taken by Erich, now an SS officer, as part of Hitler's confiscation of Jewish art. But Erich cannot bring himself to hand over the painting. As the war nears its end, he hides it in the salt mines.

Izaac, now in Auschwitz, is forced to play for the processions going into the gas chambers. When he sees his *Brundibar* cast filing past he is unable to bear it any longer and decides that he will not play again. He is rescued by Erich and they retrieve Louise's portrait.

After the war, Izaac retires to the peace of Connemara and becomes a violin teacher. He does not unwrap Louise's painting, afraid of the memories, until a young boy prompts him into playing as he once did for her. A fisherman sees Professor Abrahams on the beach, accompanied by a young woman in a green dress and a flock of children.

THE STORY OF IRELAND

Brendan O'Brien

FULL OF INFORMATION AND FUN

All you could want to know about Ireland's history

The book's 27 chapters chronicle the big picture of invasions, wars, Christianity, famine and a divided island, mixed with tales of Celtic head hunters, mysterious stone tombs, the Viking Ivar the Boneless, the Black Death, life in castles, roads, superstitions, schools and games, growing towns such as Dublin and Belfast, the *Titanic* tragedy, music, mobiles and computers.